DARING TO BE
Abigail

A Richard Jackson Book

Also by the Author

Ever After

Do-Over

Wonder

DARING TO BE
Abigail

: .

A novel by Rachel Vail

Orchard Books   *New York*

Orchard Books, 95 Madison Avenue, New York, NY 10016

Manufactured in the United States of America. Book design by Jean Krulis. The text of this book is set in 12 point Garamond Light.

10 9 8 7 6 5 4 3 2 1

Library of Congress Cataloging-in-Publication Data
Vail, Rachel. Daring to be Abigail / a novel by Rachel Vail. p.   cm. "A Richard Jackson book"—Half t.p. Summary: During her summer at Camp Nashaquitsa, eleven-year-old Abby tries to reinvent herself, while worrying about her mother, missing her dead father, and getting to know her equally self-conscious bunkmates.
ISBN 0-531-09517-7.—ISBN 0-531-08867-7 (lib. bdg.)
[1. Camps—Fiction. 2. Self-perception—Fiction. 3. Parent and child—Fiction.] I. Title.
PZ7.V1916Dar 1996   [Fic]—dc20   95-33531

To my beautiful son,

    Zachary,

    who astonishes me and explodes my heart;

and in loving memory of my gentle Grammy,

    Evelyn Silverman,

    who watches over him

DARING TO BE
Abigail

July 1

Dear Mom,

Don't worry. We'll be fine. We're already fine + we're still on the bus!

The counselor has probably unpacked my ~~trunk~~ + made my bed by now. That's weird. ~~I wish~~ I keep thinking of some stranger touching my stuff. ~~What if~~

I forgot my soap on the bathroom counter (Oooops!) Could you please send it to me? Or I'll be sooo dirty by visiting Day!!!!

Love you,
Abby

Sorry
Sloppy

But the
Bus is
Bouncing

CAMP NASHAQUITSA
ADVENTURES IN FRIENDSHIP

P.S. If you get lonely write to me.
P.P.S. Jake says hi + he's getting happier.

Abigail tried to swallow but had forgotten how.

She stood on the front step of Bunk Eleven with her fingers on the door handle, trying. Oh, great, she thought. If I can't get myself to swallow, I'll spend the entire summer spitting. That will really win people over.

She adjusted her Red Sox cap, opened the door, and stepped into the bunk. Gund bears waited patiently, arms outstretched, on scratchy wool army blankets on all the beds except two, which propped up their stuffed animals on frilly comforters and sheets of soft cotton, pretty flowers, pastels. One of these was hers.

Abigail had begged her mother for a scratchy wool army blanket. No real adventurer would have a flowered yellow comforter set, she had tried to explain. Her mother didn't think that was a good enough reason to spend thirty-nine dollars at the army-navy store. Abigail would have to learn to be brave despite the bedding she already had.

She was swinging her duffel bag onto her flowered comforter when a voice from the bed on top of hers asked, "Do you shave?"

The question caught Abigail mid-swing. She let go and the heavy bag plopped onto the floor with a thud. Abigail looked up at the two girls peering down at her and said, "Oh!" In her quick glance around the bunk she hadn't noticed them in the shadows up there; she had been distracted by her comforter.

"Shave," the girl repeated.

Abigail tried to respond. She wanted to make a good impression. She wanted to give the right answer.

"Your legs." The girl asking the question, Robin, yanked two sections of hair in her ponytail to tighten it. She was trying to find out what kind of kid Abigail was. Small, but maybe athletic, Robin thought, despite that weird thing she just did with her duffel. Robin waited for an answer.

"Me?" Abigail asked.

"No," said the other girl, Tiff. "The one next to you."

There was nobody next to Abigail. She thought maybe she should just turn around and go home; this whole camp thing wasn't working out that well.

Abigail swallowed, finally, and shook her head.

Tiff smiled, showing two neat rows of tiny teeth inside her huge mouth. A pink baby barrette pressed the frizzy black hair above her right ear into a little valley. She liked Abigail already, so nervous and quiet. "You probably don't need to shave," Tiff said, and hung her legs down over the edge of her bed. "Looks like a hairy ape, right? But my mother says not until I'm twelve."

"Oh." Abigail nodded, not sure if she should agree with this large girl that she looked like a hairy ape or say no, no, you are much less hairy than an ape. She tried to keep herself from saying "ape" at all, to be safe.

"I'm gonna do it for her," Robin said, pulling her long, muscular, shaved legs into the circle of her arms. "If you want, I can do yours, too."

Abigail clutched the Ziploc bag of oatmeal chocolate chip cookies her mother had made for her and tried to come up with a good response. "Um" was all she could manage. Her toes gripped the tube socks inside her new Adidas Superstars, size six. Abigail's feet were a size five, but she was planning to grow over the summer, and her mother had given in on this one.

"You like Twizzlers?" Robin asked, holding up an economy pack.

Abigail nodded.

"What's your name?" asked Tiff.

4

"Abby—Abigail. Silverman."

"I'm somebody and this is somebody" was all Abigail heard. She was so busy reminding herself to be Abigail instead of Abby this summer that she forgot to listen. She nodded and said hello, and when Robin invited her up onto the bed for a Twizzler, Abigail climbed the ladder.

"You like oatmeal chocolate chip cookies?" Abigail asked on her way up. She hadn't eaten any of the fourteen cookies on the bus, in fact had been determined to ration them, one a day for the first two weeks, to remember the taste of home.

Tiff took two cookies and said, "You can call me Tiff. I'm too big to be a Tiffany. My mother I think wanted somebody little like you, and cute, is why she named me that."

You're little, Abigail thought of reassuring huge Tiff, or, You're cute, or, I'm sure your mother is happy with what she got. Instead she took a Twizzler and shoved it quickly into her mouth to block anything stupid from coming out, and handed her Ziploc bag to Robin, who helped herself to one cookie.

"You're new," Robin said to Abigail, as she took a bite. She studied Abigail with pale green eyes under bushy blond eyebrows.

Abigail wanted very much to be liked by her. "Yeah," she said. "Were you both here last year?"

Robin nodded and took another bite. "Scared?"

"No," Abigail said too quickly. A piece of Twizzler went down the wrong way and she started to cough.

"You okay?" Tiff asked.

Abigail nodded, though tears were coming into her eyes. She grabbed her legs and pulled them in like Robin. "My little brother cried, on the bus."

"That's so embarrassing," Tiff said, grabbing another cookie from Abigail's bag.

"He's only eight." Abigail felt she had to defend Jake, now that she had betrayed him.

"Still," said Tiff, chewing.

"I told him camp is for learning to be brave, but he kept crying."

"That's so cute," Tiff said. "Camp is for learning to be brave. I love that."

Robin handed Abigail another Twizzler and said, "Last year I was so scared, I forgot my mitt. My mother had to FedEx it."

"I forgot my soap," Abigail admitted.

"It gets better," said Robin softly. She had decided. She liked a person who would try to comfort her little brother.

"You can share mine," Tiff said. "It's Ivory. Very pure."

"Thanks," said Abigail. She leaned back against the wood paneling and scratched her head by shifting the brim of the Red Sox cap, her father's old one. She had grabbed it during her last look around her room before leaving for the camp bus, and was now planning to wear it until she went home again. She was going to reinvent herself this summer. She had already started.

A short girl with a perfect bowl haircut and a Camp Nashaquitsa T-shirt flung open the door and stepped inside. As it slammed shut behind her, she grinned and said, "Hi! I'm Dana!"

"Do you shave?" Robin asked.

"That's the funniest question," Dana said. "Hold on, I just have to figure out, oh, I guess this is me, here." She plopped her pink suitcase onto the only other bed with a matching comforter and sheets. Abigail smiled at her for having that in common, and wondered if they'd become best friends. Abigail was hoping for a best friend, and obviously Tiff and Robin were already taken by each other.

"Do you shave? Hey!"

"No, I mean, it's so funny because my best friend at home? Roberta but we call her Bobbi?" Oh, well, Abigail thought. She's taken, too. "Bobbi's always doing surveys like that, like asking everybody in the cafeteria do you shampoo first or wash, things like that? And then writing it up for the school paper? We go to a special school for gifted children? My IQ is one-forty-five. You're not supposed to know, but I found the paper in my mother's night table drawer?"

Robin tightened her ponytail and said, "It wasn't a survey."

"My name is Dana," Dana said. "Did I tell you that already? I'm a yellow belt in Tae Kwon Do, and I won first prize in Rhode Island for baton twirling. I practice six hours every day?"

"Why?" asked Robin.

"What a waste of time," Tiff said, shaking her head at Abigail.

"It's very good exercise," said Dana.

"It's very good exercise," mocked Tiff.

Dana turned around, pulled her T-shirts out of her cubby, and started refolding them. Abigail wanted to invite her to come up on the top bunk, even if she did have a best friend somewhere else. She could tell Dana was nervous. It's scary down there alone on the floor, looking up at people who already seem so in, Abigail remembered from a minute earlier. But this wasn't her bed. She didn't say anything.

"Is that gum?" Tiff pointed over to Dana's cubby.

"Yeah," said Dana.

"Aren't you gonna share?"

Dana picked up the pack and pulled the little red ribbon out of it, then worked open the tinfoil. It took a long time. Abigail sat between Robin and Tiff on the top bunk, watching. Dana carefully pulled out two pieces, bent them each in half, then ripped precisely down the middles. She handed each of the girls half a piece and kept one half for herself.

"Half a piece?" Robin asked.

"It has to last the whole summer," Dana explained, placing the gum in her mouth and the wrapper, folded, in her pocket. "Besides, if you chew a whole piece at once, you get big cheek muscles."

"Oh, my goodness gracious," Tiff said, slapping herself on the face. "I would just about die if I ever got big cheek muscles."

"That's not true," said Robin. She had decided about Dana by now, too. "It's how much chewing you do, not the size of the piece. That doesn't make any sense."

Tiff grabbed Abigail by the shoulders. "Abigail. Promise me if I ever get big cheek muscles, you'll lock me in a closet and never let me out."

Abigail unwrapped her half-piece, popped it in her mouth, and threw her crumpled-up wrapper at Tiff, who laughed and threw hers down at Dana. Dana didn't laugh. She picked up the wrapper and put it in her pocket, then went and rearranged her T-shirt pile again.

July 1 again

Dear Mom,

Other kids have Army blankets. I told you. Oh — never mind sending my soap. I'm sharing.

Who's going to say "Have a nice day I love you" to me tomorrow? I miss you but now I have to go for a swim test. Hope I get in deep!!!

Have a nice day. I love you.

Abby

P.S. Can I shave?

The high diving board loomed above the pool, like a dare. Abigail spotted it as they were heading down to swim, and pushed the memory of that other high dive out of her head. I'm in camp now, she told herself. These kids don't know me. I could be anyone.

She listened to the thwack of flip-flops hitting soles of feet as they trudged down the pebbly hill, and hoped hers wouldn't pop apart, as flip-flops sometimes do, sending the foot crashing forward so the sole gets scraped. She gripped with her toes. Her towel was bristly on her bare shoulders, and her bathing cap felt like a month-old balloon, limp in her hand. She kept up the pace, in the middle of this group of strangers she was going to live with for the next eight weeks. She wondered if any of them had noticed her skinny, flat-chested body as she changed, even though she had kept her T-shirt on and her eyes lowered the whole time. As they approached the pool area, the girl next to her, Tracy, clicked her retainer against the top of her mouth a few times. Abigail wished she had a retainer, or gum, or a talent. Something to rest comfortably against.

Kat, the counselor, swung the gate open, and the girls filed into the pool area. The wind was blowing in gusts; if Abigail were home, at the club, her mother would say it was too cold for swimming, why not read a book on a lounge chair instead? She looked at the grim faces of the other girls. The first test of the summer, she thought.

"You like those?" Tracy asked.

Abigail had been standing near the NO RUNNING sign, staring blankly at the diving board. She blinked and pretended to shiver, in what she hoped was a friendly way. "High dives?"

"Because you were staring."

"Oh," said Abigail. "Um, not really. Do you?"

"No way," Tracy whispered, and went to hang her towel behind the bench and sit down. She sat with her hands under her skinny thighs, palms down against the wood bench. Abigail smiled to herself; she did that, too. It kept thighs from spreading and looking huge.

Abigail wrapped herself in her towel and sat down next to Tracy. "It's cold."

"Yeah." Tracy rocked slightly on her hands and focused on the deep end.

Abigail counted the steps up to the high dive.

Twelve. Not so many. She wondered how many steps went up to the one at the club, and guessed twice that many. At least, that's how it had felt, that day with her father.

Tiff cannonballed into the pool, splashing Abigail and Tracy and most of the other campers. "Freezing!" she screamed. Robin did a racing dive from the shallow end. The slim swim lady ran toward the shallow end, yelling, "No diving!" Robin was still underwater, though, like a perfect straight arrow, heading toward Deep.

"I thought no running," Tracy whispered to Abigail, and Abigail smiled again. She had been thinking that, too.

Dana stood on the steps in the shallow end, dipping her wrists in. "This helps you get used to it," she said to Heather, who was pushing stray tufts of hair into her swim cap and not paying any attention to Dana. "Really, it's scientifically proven, because of pulse points?" Heather adjusted the straps of her bikini top, slipped gracefully into the water up to her neck, and swam away. Dana grinned and said to nobody in particular, "I read about it somewhere. An article."

Twelve steps up, thought Abigail. Not impossible. I could climb up those twelve steps and jump off that board into the pool, and these girls would think that was just the kind of person I am.

Nancy sat on the edge and dangled her feet in the pool. "Kat?" she asked. "If we just want to be in Shallow, is that okay? Do we have to take the test?"

Kat sat down beside Nancy and put her arm around her. "Don't you even want to try? It's just a lap."

"There and back, right?"

"That counts as one."

"I don't like to put my face in. It makes me suffocate."

"Okay," said Kat. "You don't have to if you don't want to. Sit by me on the bench. But I bet by the end of the summer you're ready for the Olympics." She clapped Nancy on the back with her big, meaty hand. It almost knocked delicate little Nancy into the pool. Kat laughed encouragingly. She planned to fill all her letters to friends with details about toughening up the girls she called "my kids." "My kids are always the toughest in the camp by the end of the summer," Kat told Nancy, and headed toward the deep end, where Robin was doing a flip turn.

Nancy said, "Oh," politely and hunched over, gripping the edge and fluttering her feet.

"Well, may as well," Tracy whispered. She pulled her bathing cap over her head and shoved in the extra hairs, then walked to the edge of the pool and, balancing on one foot, dipped her toes in. "Cold," she mouthed to Abigail, who was still sitting on the bench with her hands propping up her thighs. Abigail nodded, hung her Red Sox cap on the fence, and tugged her bathing cap down onto her hair.

Tracy clamped her fingers over her nose and jumped in. Abigail had been hoping Tracy would wait for her, that they would go down the steps together slowly, getting used to it. She didn't really want to be stuck on the steps with Dana, who was grinning at nobody and looking for someone to tell about pulse points and articles she'd read. Abigail knew how Dana felt, and was tempted to go and save her from the humiliating feeling of being caught in the middle of telling a story to everybody's back. But this summer, Abigail thought, that will not happen to me. These girls don't know. They might think I'm popular at home, and daring.

She couldn't remember the climb up, that time at the club, or why she had decided to try it. She couldn't even remember if her parents had really forbidden it, or if it had just been so inconceivable that such a fearful kid would *want* to go off the high dive that they had never discussed it. She could picture her father down in the pool pulling Jake around in his floaties, and her mother, in a lounge chair next to Mrs. Bender, chatting. Nobody had been looking at her, and the high dive was suddenly irresistible. All the bigger kids were climbing up, diving or jumping off, and then she was up there, on the edge. The sounds of the big kids seemed far away, but she did hear Jake down in the pool say, "Hey, look! Abby!" He pointed up at her. Her father looked up, her mother looked up, Mrs. Bender looked up. Abby looked down, down, down into the pool, which seemed centuries away.

Her father had lifted Jake out of the pool and yelled, "C'mon, then, Abigail!"

"What are you, nuts?" her mother shrieked. "Abby, turn around and climb back down the ladder."

There were kids behind her, waiting. They'll let me pass through, Abigail remembered telling herself. She was about to turn around and climb down to the warm safety of her mother's tan body when she heard her father yell, "Don't be a wimp!"

The words forced her into the air as absolutely as if he had stood behind her and pushed.

She didn't jump so much as discover herself in the air, having jumped, at which point it was too late to reconsider. There was just enough time to take a breath before the water slapped her body with such angry, punishing spite she felt she had splintered into millions of tiny shards.

"I'm proud of you," her father whispered, his strong hands gathering her together under the water. She sagged against him. Then he lifted her out of the pool into the greedy arms of her mother, who scooped her in and held her, tight and safe and protected.

That was three summers ago. She'd taken the shallow-end steps every time since then.

And now she was on the edge of a different pool, away at camp and eleven years old. Not one person here knew what a wimp she really was. Tiff hoisted herself out of the water and threatened, "Jump by three or I'll throw you in!" She grinned at Abigail. With all her bushy hair compressed into the tight bathing cap, Tiff looked like an overgrown toddler—happy, eager, with pudgy cheeks and a bit of defiance.

"One . . ."

"I'm going."

"Two!"

"No pushing," Kat said, coming to stand beside Tiff.

"Two and a half . . ."

Abigail gasped and was in the air. She hadn't decided whether to dive or jump and so was heading for the water belly first.

For the second time in her life, Abigail regretted her inability to remain in the air forever. She knew that what was about to happen would hurt and that there was nothing she could do now to stop it. The choice had been made, and she was falling fast toward the consequences.

Dear Mom,

Hi! How are you? I'm fine. Thanks for the letter. I love mail. Here are the answers to your ?s:

The girls in my bunk are

Tiff - funny & lovable and gorgeous! ← Tiff wrote that

Robin - a jock, a twin, serious

Tracy - like Eliza Smith at home - you know - everybody wants to sit next to her

Heather - has pierced ears + diamond chip cat earrings acts grown up

Dana - stands too close when she talks, smart, tries too hard

Nancy - little pretty, homesick

Me - ???

The counselor is: Rat - tough but nice

The food is: Fine. Not vegetarian. Actually gross

The activities: Great!!

The weather: Great!!

Everything else: Great !!!!!!!

P.S. The water fountain water smells like rotten eggs.

PPS it got in Deep!

Do you miss me?

Love your daughter Ally

+ 2 good
2 be
4 gotten

The inside folds of Abigail's elbows were beginning to itch desperately. Tiff told her it was because
she was so clean from using her Ivory. Abigail scratched
her neck, then behind her knees, and said that was
probably true. She wasn't convinced, though, and while
she was washing her hands again at the middle sink,
bending under Nancy, who was brushing her shiny
black hair, she started thinking that if she got much
cleaner she would go insane with itchiness.

Abigail was trying to become as clean and pretty
as possible for Brother-Sister Night because Tiff had
explained that it was really a Social. Heather and Tracy
were putting on makeup together at the first sink. Robin
sat on her bed, playing catch by herself with her softball
and mitt. Dana was using mouthwash at the third sink,
which Tiff thought was hilarious. She asked if she could
borrow some and then imitated Dana's gurgles.
Heather laughed, so Tiff did it again; Tiff could sense

the girls enjoying her joke but feeling slightly afraid of her—a strong combination—and also figured it couldn't hurt to have minty breath for the Social.

"What do you say, ladies?" Kat yelled.

Abigail quickly flipped her hair, put her Red Sox cap back on, and ran to wait by the cabin door. At the Bunk Get-to-Know-One-Another the first night, Kat had told them she wasn't about to tolerate any crap from a bunch of flat-chested eleven-year-olds, so watch your step. Tiff said counselors weren't allowed to beat up campers, but Abigail wasn't taking any chances.

Everybody else got to the door in a matter of seconds, too, and together they headed down to Olympic Hall, across the bridge, on Boys' Side.

"She doesn't scare me," Tracy whispered to Abigail.

"Me neither," Abigail whispered back, forcing herself not to look up at the high dive as they passed the pool area.

Tiff caught up with them and asked, "You want to know the trick to getting asked out?"

It was dark on the stone steps; the light bulbs were hung only every few yards. The crickets were chirping, and the night smelled like pine. Abigail looked at Tracy and they both nodded, happy to be trusted with the secrets of an experienced camper.

"Whatever you do," Tiff warned, "don't go right up into the canteen line."

"Okay," Tracy whispered.

Abigail stifled the urge to ask why not going right up to canteen would make a boy like her. She watched Tracy kick a stone down the steps and thought, *She knows how to act.* Like all the most popular girls at school, Tracy *whispers.* So Abigail whispered, "Okay," too.

"If somebody asks you out, he'll buy you something after," Tiff explained. "You know, to make it official. Nobody is going to ask you out if you already have a pack of peanut M&M's."

They were crossing the bridge by then, and the lights of Boys' Side illuminated the lake. Tracy clicked her retainer against the top of her mouth and said, "Why would he?"

"Exactly," said Tiff. She pushed her hair down, hoping it wouldn't look too frizzy for a boy to accept. If she couldn't be pretty, she kept telling herself, she would try to be knowledgeable and funny. Maybe that would make people like her, even though she had heard her mother telling her father that Tiff would never have it easy, because of the way she looked. She slumped her broad shoulders and tried to seem smaller.

They stepped through the wide doorway of Olympic Hall together. Abigail looked up at the dozens of flags hanging from the ceiling and imagined herself standing again in the same spot on the last day of the summer, having become as magnetic as Tracy and as likable as Tiff.

When Jake saw Abigail, relief loosened his tense face, and he ran over to stand with her and Tiff, under the flag of Ecuador. Tracy kept walking, and Abigail lost sight of her in the swirl of freshly shampooed campers. Heather, who was wearing short-shorts, a halter, and sandals, stood next to Tiff. She looked down at Jake and made a sound like "Tst," but Jake didn't care. He wasn't budging.

"How's your bunk?" Abigail asked Jake.

"Okay," he said, staring at Heather. "Is she your counselor?"

"No, a kid. Do you like the boys in your bunk?"

He shrugged. "She's pretty."

Heather scanned Olympic Hall, pretending not to hear the compliment. She hoped some older boys would agree with this intense-looking little kid.

"Do they like you?" Abigail asked Jake.

"No," he said.

"Why not?"

"Because I cheat."

Heather couldn't help smiling. Abigail decided she didn't like Heather very much. The thing she had told about herself the first night was that her rug at home had "Heather" spelled out on it in script, and there was a step up to her bed area.

"They already found out you cheat?" Abigail asked. Jake nodded.

"Well, that's why I don't like to play with you."

"Yeah," said Jake. "Also because sometimes I sit on the box tops and break them. You hate that, too."

"Maybe you should try not cheating," Abigail suggested. "And sit right on the floor, like everybody else."

"Oh," he said. "Okay."

"That's your brother?" asked Heather. Abigail wished Jake had stayed home like he'd wanted to.

"No," said Tiff. "Her uncle."

"Tst," said Heather. Abigail smiled at Tiff and put her arm around Jake.

Robin ran up and grabbed Abigail by the shoulders. "Do you like that boy over there?" She pointed across the room.

"That one?"

"Yeah."

"With the blond hair?"

"No, gross. The tall one with brown." Robin moved behind Abigail and pointed again, over Abigail's shoulder. "Sort of dorky-looking but cute?"

Abigail leaned to her left, trying to get a good look. "I don't know."

"He wants to know if you like him," Robin said, stepping into Abigail's line of vision. She was impatient, wanted an answer, yes or no.

"I guess so," Abigail said. "What's his name?"

"Scott, I think. If he asked you out, would you say yes?"

Abigail squinted around Robin but still couldn't make out his features very clearly. "I guess," she said.

"I thought boys are disgusting," said Jake.

"Shhh." Abigail pushed Jake behind her and scratched her knee.

Robin sprinted back across Olympic Hall to the boys.

"The blond one is her twin, Caleb," said Tiff, motioning with her chin. "That's how she can go over and talk to the boys without everybody hating her for being a total flirt. Don't they look exactly alike?"

"Not really," said Abigail. Robin was taller and skinnier than Caleb, and had much darker blond hair.

"I can never tell them apart," Tiff joked.

Abigail caught on. "Actually, are you sure he's not *your* twin? He looks exactly like you!"

"Like Tiff? No way," said Heather. "He's so ... little." Abigail could tell Heather almost said "cute." The thing Tiff had told about herself was "I'm prettier than I look."

"Separated at birth," Tiff said. "If you go out with that boy, you have to kiss him, you know."

"Yeah?" Abigail scratched her arm, where little bumps were beginning to appear.

24

Robin came back over and said very formally, "Scott wants to know if you'll go out with him."

"I dare you," Tiff said.

The thing Abigail had told about herself when they went around the circle was that she never said no to a dare. It was true, technically. She just didn't mention that she'd never been dared to do anything before. "Yes," Abigail said.

Robin faced the boys and made an okay sign. Scott, Abigail's new boyfriend, jammed his hands down into his shorts pockets and turned around. Heather said, "Your boyfriend has a cute butt."

"Thank you," said Abigail.

That was it, they were going out. Abigail's boyfriend and Robin's brother went over to where some other boys were throwing around a Nerf football.

"She didn't even get any M&M's," Tiff complained.

"Maybe next time," said Robin, apologetically.

"It doesn't matter," Abigail said, relieved she didn't have to kiss.

Abigail took Jake over to his counselor when Uncle Gary, the head of camp, blew a whistle and announced that it was time for the lower camps to go back to their bunks. Although in fact he had no nieces or nephews of his own, Uncle Gary did look like an uncle. He had white hair, soft blue eyes, rosy cheeks, and what Tiff called a "perma-grin." Smiling broadly in the center of

Olympic Hall, Uncle Gary half listened to Dana while keeping a watchful eye on how the counselors were rounding up their groups. He wore his Camp Nashaquitsa shirt tight and his white knee socks pulled all the way up, and had spent every spring for the past seventeen years memorizing each camper's full name, parent's name or names, and hometown. He believed that his awareness comforted homesick children, and that the effort he exerted earned him the title of Uncle. "Send my best to Rhoda and Bill in Barrington," he called to Dana as he sauntered away, leaving her standing alone.

Bunk Eleven was gathering around Kat under the Swiss flag, so Dana ran over and they headed out. Tracy whispered to Abigail as they crossed the creaky porch that she had been asked out, too, and that her new boyfriend, Oliver, had bought her a Milky Way. "That's excellent," Abigail whispered back.

Nancy had said yes to a boy whose name she had been too shy to ask, she told everybody as they were crossing the bridge, because he had picked up a bug on the floor and taken it outside. Nancy admired that because she believed bugs have rights, too. That made Kat laugh. "Sounds like true love."

"Yeah," Nancy said. "Maybe I'll marry whatever his name is someday because we have that in common and most boys would step on a bug." Tracy rolled her eyes. She went to school with Nancy at home and had requested that they be put in different bunks.

"Congratulations," Dana said to Abigail as they walked up the rocky steps toward Girls' Side. "You must be so excited."

Abigail shrugged, then admitted, "Yeah."

Dana slung her arm across Abigail's shoulders and started telling stories about her boyfriend at home, how cute he was, how smart, how much they loved each other. Abigail didn't mind Dana's chatter; she smiled and nodded and said, "That's great, Dana." But she wasn't really listening. She was smiling up at the looming high dive, thinking about the fact that a boy had looked across a crowded room and picked her.

July 11

Dear Mom,

Hi. How are you? I'm fine. Camp is great!!!! I saw Jake at Brother-Sister night. He's having a great time, too. See? Nothing to worry about.

I have a boyfriend!!!!!! And a rash. His name is Scott. (The boyfriend.)

SWAK!
Abby

Dana was dustpan and Abigail was first sweep. Abigail was proud that they got a ten on inspection of the floor, too, but she wished Dana would shut up about it already. She looked over at Heather and Robin, who had been dustpan and first sweep the day before, when they got a six. Robin kicked Dana's bed the third time Dana said to Abigail, "We make a great team, huh?"

"Yeah," Abigail said, going into the bathroom. Dana followed her in, so Abigail went into a stall and locked the door. Dana leaned against it.

"I was thinking? Since we're both in Deep? Wanna be buddies at swim?"

"Everybody got in Deep."

"Except Nancy," Dana corrected.

"I already promised Tracy," Abigail lied. She pulled down her shorts and sat there, wishing Dana would leave. She didn't.

29

"Tomorrow, then? Wanna be buddies tomorrow?"

Abigail pulled up her shorts and flushed. "Sure," she said, on her way to the sink. She couldn't say she had already made plans for the whole summer.

"Great," said Dana, standing so close Abigail could smell the Scope on her breath. "Maybe we'll play Marco Polo. I'm a premier Marco Polo player."

Abigail nodded as she pushed past Dana and went over to sit on Tracy's bed. She leaned toward Tracy and whispered in her ear, "We're buddies for swim. I just told Dana."

"You're so mean," Tracy said. Abigail wondered if that was true. Tracy laughed. "I think that's what I like best about you. That or your haircut."

"I did it myself," Abigail said. "The bangs."

"No kidding." Tracy smiled. "Are you homesick?"

"No." Abigail pulled her Red Sox cap forward to hide the bangs better. "Are you?"

"Yeah," Tracy whispered. She had rolled her eyes the first night of camp when Nancy cried, so that no-body would think she felt the same way. But after Kat had rubbed Nancy's back until she was asleep and all the other campers had settled into their beds again, Tracy had hidden under her pillow, whispering "Mommy" into the fur of her Gund bear.

She flipped her hair out of her face and smiled at Abigail, to show she wasn't desperate. "I shouldn't be homesick," Tracy said, with a laugh in her voice, she hoped. "All my parents do is fight, and my great-grandmother chews so you can see the food, and has a pacemaker, so we can't get a microwave."

"Wait," said Abigail. "Why can't you get a microwave?"

"Because Bubby would blow up."

"No way." The thing Tracy had told about herself was that her great-grandmother lived with them at home and always changed her clothes in the closet.

"Seriously. The doctor said. If you have a pacemaker and somebody turns on a microwave, you explode."

"Wow," said Abigail, wondering how many great-grandmothers had exploded before doctors figured out the connection.

"Yeah. I mean, I have to love her because she's related and everything, but personally I'd rather have a microwave."

"I have one," said Abigail. "They're not that great."

"Yeah, well. I couldn't wait to get away from all that, and now ..." She reached over and twirled Abigail's shoelace between her fingers, afraid she had admitted too much already. "Don't tell anybody, though," she whispered. "I'll get over it."

"Okay," said Abigail.

Tracy touched the brim of Abigail's cap. "It's cool

that you like the Red Sox. My dad's into the Yankees, so he hates the Sox. I root for them just to get back at him. For whatever. Everything. You know."

"Yeah. It's my father's hat," Abigail said. "We both love them. Want an oatmeal chocolate chip cookie?" She had only one left, but Tracy seemed to need it.

"Okay."

Abigail grabbed the Ziploc bag off her cubby and handed it to Tracy.

"Aren't you glad you're not Dana?" Tracy asked, biting into the cookie.

"Yeah."

"I mean, nobody likes her." Tracy handed the cookie to Abigail, who took a bite and handed it back. While Tracy was finishing the cookie, Abigail looked over to where Dana was sitting alone on her fancy comforter, holding the baton that so far she had not once practiced twirling. Tiff and Robin were playing "spit" on Tiff's bed, and across the bunk Heather was allowing Nancy to try her kissing-potion lip gloss.

"Yeah," whispered Abigail, avoiding Dana's eyes by brushing crumbs off Tracy's army blanket. "That must feel terrible."

July 19

Dear Mom,

My rash keeps getting worse & worse. I might be allergic to Ivory because I can't stop scratching. Don't worry I went to the infirmary & they put grass goo on it 2x a day. Maybe you better ~~send~~ FedEx my Dove.

Answers to your ?'s: Scott ~~is~~ seems really nice. His interests are Sports. ~~and~~ My best friend—Tracy. My best activity—Swim.

She has the bluest eyes you ever saw plus a great-grandmother.

Love & other indoor sports,
Abley

PS Did you sign up for any of those classes? I really think you should. Maybe pottery. You like pots.

PPS Sorry I haven't written more. Don't be sad or worried. I'll try to be better. This is a longie, huh? But camp is so busy (In a good way) They keep us running from activity to activity. No resting or thinking. It's so fun!!!!!!!!!

When Abigail heard the rain pounding on the roof the next morning, her first feeling was relief that she wouldn't have to be buddies with Dana at swim. But then, quickly, she regretted the feeling and tried to deny to herself that she had experienced it. She was afraid that if she allowed herself to have a nasty thought, something bad would happen as punishment—nobody would be buddies with Jake at swim, for instance, or her mother would die in a car accident.

After breakfast and inspection, Kat suggested a jacks tournament. Heather was winning and Abigail hadn't even gotten up to fancies despite the fact that her mother had practiced with her all through June. She and Dana were the worst jacks players in the bunk. A minute after Kat left to try to find some bingo cards, Dana got a splinter.

"Maybe I'll go to the infirmary after lunch," she said.

"For a splinter?" asked Robin.

"What a baby," said Tiff. "I'll take it out with a pin." She lit the lighter she kept hidden under her T-shirts and held the flame on a safety pin she took from Nancy's sewing kit. "Maybe I'll go to the infirmary," she mocked quietly while she sterilized.

"You never tease Abigail when she goes to the infirmary," said Dana. "Right, Abigail?"

"Look at me," said Abigail, blushing. She did not want to get caught in the middle of this. She held up her arm and showed the rash inside her elbow. "I'm gross. All you have is a splinter."

Tiff laughed. "You are gross."

"It's your soap," Tracy said quickly. At home Tracy always felt it was her job to make a joke or lighten the mood to keep her parents from fighting. She had planned on camp being a break, a rest, but she sensed a fight brewing here, just as her great-grandmother's arthritic fingers could anticipate rain.

"A splinter is at least as serious as a rash," said Dana. "I'm going to the infirmary. Don't even think of coming near me with that pin, or I'll scream." She glared at Tiff, who glared right back, pin in one hand and lighter in the other. Abigail held her breath and wondered if they would punch each other.

Tracy scooped up the jacks and ball and dropped them into her little plastic jacks bag. "Sooo," she said. "That's enough jacks, huh? Too violent a sport for me."

Tiff broke the staring contest with Dana and laughed. "Yeah. It's always funny until someone gets hurt."

"Somebody could lose an eye," Heather added.

"This kind of laughing turns into crying," Tracy said, imitating a grown-up voice.

"If your friends jumped off a bridge ..." Abigail started.

"Would you?" everybody, even Dana, answered. They all giggled. Abigail sighed. Tracy clicked her retainer a few times.

Heather flopped down on her bed and said, "I like jacks."

"How about Marco Polo?" Nancy suggested.

"That's a water game, space cadet," Robin said. She picked up her ball and mitt to have a little catch with herself until somebody came up with a better idea.

"I'm a premier Marco Polo player," said Dana. "At home I—"

"We could play it here, though," said Tracy. "Sort of like blindman's buff combined with freeze tag."

"Yeah!" Tiff yelled.

Nancy smiled. Usually Tracy ignored her.

Tiff tossed the safety pin and lighter onto the top of her cubby and grabbed one of her ten bandannas. She wore them as headbands sometimes.

Tracy whispered to Abigail, "Don't get me and I

won't get you." Abigail nodded, thinking of all the times at school she wasn't the one being whispered to, and how much better this felt.

"One potato two potato to see who's it," Tiff said, so they all stood up and put their fists into the center. Abigail won. Or lost. Tiff tied the bandanna around her eyes so tightly she saw orange.

"Tight enough?"

"Youch," Abigail said. Tiff loosened it a bit.

"Okay, can you see?"

"No. I swear." Abigail adjusted the bandanna so it wouldn't flatten her nose. If she left it that way, she could see a shadow of floor so she wouldn't trip and make a fool of herself. She moved it back down. Nobody will play with Jake because he cheats, she reminded herself.

"Okay," Tiff said. "We can run till you say Marco, then we freeze and say Polo, and you try to catch us."

"Okay," Abigail said. "Marco!" She reached out and grabbed just as everybody yelled Polo, and somebody's arm was in her hands. She took off the bandanna, hoping it wasn't Tracy, since she had promised not to catch her. It was Dana. Her skin felt as soft as the inside of a brand-new sweatshirt.

"Wait," Dana said. "I didn't know we were starting."

"Tough tamales," said Robin. "Play by the rules. Dana's it."

37

"That was too easy." Tiff plucked another bandanna, a pink one, off her heap. "Let's tie her hands."

Abigail was already tying the first bandanna gently around Dana's eyes. Tiff took Dana's hands and yanked them behind her back.

"How is she supposed to grab us?" asked Nancy.

"We'll be frozen, dummy," Robin said. "She can stick out her leg or shoulder or whatever and touch us."

"Oh," Nancy said. She bent over to touch her toes, the way she had learned in ballet class. Being called dummy always made Nancy want to cry, whether it was Robin saying it or her older sister, Ruth. She never knew how to make her parents discuss things seriously with her as they did with Ruth, instead of changing the subject every time she talked. She had hoped that in camp things would be different, that she would be in the center of the action instead of shoved to the side. She kissed her knees, pulling the stretch until it hurt.

"Is that all right?" Abigail asked Dana.

"Yeah," she said. "I guess. Thanks."

She looked like a hostage waiting to be shot. Everybody started to run.

"Marco?" Dana said, nervously. She shuffled toward Abigail and Tracy, who were trapped near Dana's bed.

"Polo!" yelled the rest of the girls.

"Marco?"

Abigail jumped over the bed and headed toward the bathroom. Dana slammed into the frame, trying blindly to follow her.

"Polo!" the girls answered.

"Ow!" Dana howled at the same time. "You guys? Time out, I hurt my toe." She tried to wriggle out of the bandannas but couldn't. She sat down on the floor.

"Waa," said Robin. "Say Marco."

"I mean it! Time out!"

"Waa! Crybaby," Tiff yelled, waving for everybody to join her in the bathroom. "Say Marco!"

The girls tiptoed in, past Dana.

"Fine," Dana said. "Marco."

Tiff put her finger to her lips. Nobody made a sound.

"Marco!"

Heather clamped her hand over her mouth to keep from laughing.

"You guys! You have to say Polo! Marco! Marco!"

Abigail had to pee but couldn't move. She stared at Dana, sitting with her legs splayed out and her hands tied behind her in the middle of the floor, facing everybody without seeing.

"Marco!" She was beginning to cry.

This is the kind of thing kids do to Jake, Abigail thought, and it kills him. I have to stop this. She didn't move.

Dana got up on her knees and crawled along the

floor until she bumped into Heather's bed. She rubbed her face on Heather's army blanket, trying to get the bandanna off. "Could somebody please help me?"

Abigail and Tracy looked at each other. If Tracy goes to help her, Abigail decided, I'll go. I'll go, too.

"Please! Somebody!"

One of Dana's hands sprang free, and she ripped the bandanna off her eyes. She blinked a couple of times at the girls huddled tight in the bathroom doorway before burying her face in the blanket.

July 20

Dear Mom,

When am I going to learn adventure stuff?
I came to camp to learn courage. It's been
almost 3 weeks and so far all I've learned is
Macrame and Marco Polo. I thought at camp I'd
learn to be brave,   to trek through the woods
at night and survive by knowing which berries
are poison and which side of the tree moss
grows on.

But Camp is really fun!!!!! I really love it.
Don't worry.
   Hope you're having fun, too.
   Gotta go!!!
      Love
      Abby

P.S. Did you decide yet if I can shave?

After bingo, Kat told Bunk Eleven that the half hour until lunch was letter-writing time. Dana finished her letter first and walked out the back door into the rain with her baton. She hadn't said a word since Marco Polo, not even "Bingo!" when all her "I" spaces were covered, two numbers before Nancy filled in the diagonal on her card and won.

Tiff finished writing next. She tucked her blanket in on one side and let the other hang down, to make Abigail's bed a fort. Abigail folded her letter and shoved it into an envelope as Tiff, Robin, and Tracy crawled behind Tiff's blanket to huddle on Abigail's flowered comforter.

"If Dana tells Kat that we ganged up and tortured her," Tiff whispered gravely, "the whole bunk could get docked."

"It's true," Robin agreed. "Last year Bunk Thirteen kept calling one kid Stuffing and they couldn't go to Evening Activity for a week."

"I think Abigail should talk to her," Tracy whispered.

"Me?"

Abigail shook her head at Tracy, who leaned across her crossed legs toward Tiff and whispered, "She likes Abigail best."

"That's true," Robin said.

They all turned to Abigail, who rolled her eyes the way Tracy always did. They didn't stop waiting, so Abigail heard herself say, "Okay." She wasn't completely sure what she was agreeing to, but the dampness in the air was combining with the smell of Tiff's wool blanket to make her feel cramped and dizzy. She bolted from the fort and changed out of her Superstars into her flip-flops for the walk down to lunch next to Dana.

Abigail watched the high dive as they approached it, and wondered if she would have the courage before the end of the summer to dive off it. She had been as far as the steps, but instead of climbing up she had swung around and cannonballed in like Tiff. Definitely before the end of the summer, she had sworn to herself underwater, her eyes open and stinging as she stared at the kicking legs of the other campers, but she hadn't chosen diving for elective again yet. Camp is for learning to be brave, she reminded herself, but the words sounded stupid and childish, so she pushed them out of her head and turned to Dana to ask, "Are you going to tell?"

Dana didn't answer at first, just kept trudging through the drizzle down the stone steps to the Dining Hall.

"Maybe," Dana finally said.

Abigail nodded. Part of her felt like saying, "Good for you, you should tell." Instead she asked, "What does it depend on?"

"I don't know. Do you think we'll have boating after lunch?"

"If it clears up. Yeah."

"Wanna take out a canoe together?"

"Oh," said Abigail. "Okay. Sure. I guess."

"Great," said Dana.

"It was just a joke, you know."

Dana nodded.

"And, as a friend, I think if you tell, things will only get worse for you." Abigail pulled on the brim of her cap to avoid looking in Dana's face. She wasn't sure if she was threatening Dana or helping her. "You know?"

"If they *could* get worse."

Abigail chuckled, relieved to hear Dana joke about it. "Well, they wouldn't get better. But if you don't tell, I think people would like that." Abigail kicked a rock as they got to the bottom of the steps, and saw it plunk into the water. As they crossed the bridge, she watched the circles it made grow bigger and bigger before she turned back to Dana. "Anyway, Tiff said if you tell, the whole bunk will get docked."

"What does that mean?"

"I don't know," Abigail admitted. "Won't it be good next year, when we're not new anymore?"

Dana smiled. "Yeah." She pushed the hood of her slicker off her head. "I think it's stopping. I'm really good at canoeing?"

"Great," Abigail said.

For lunch there was something called Hockey Pucks. Tiff and Robin were so excited, they each grabbed two of the steaming hot disks off the platter with their fingers. Abigail tried to stab one with her fork but couldn't pierce it. She picked it up and bit in. She chewed and chewed and kept on chewing, but nothing was happening. "Yuck," she said, trying to swallow. "Pass the peanut butter."

"You're crazy, these are great," Tiff said with her mouth full.

"Kat?" Dana poked at her Hockey Puck. "What does it mean if you get docked?"

Tiff stopped chewing. Robin put down her Hockey Puck. Heather's hand hung in front of the ketchup.

"It means no Evening Activity. You sit in the bunk and stare at the walls all night. Why?"

"And why would somebody get docked?"

"If you don't do what I tell you, something like that. Like getting punished at home. You know? Why?"

"When I'm punished at home," Dana said, "I get a time-out and sit in my room without dinner."

"Same concept," said Kat. "You gonna use that ketchup, Heather, or wave at it?"

Heather passed Kat the ketchup.

"My mother hits me with a wooden spoon," Tiff said. She smiled at Dana. "You're lucky."

"Really? Hits you? Where?"

"On the butt, if I'm lucky. Plenty of padding there."

"My father slapped me across the face once," said Tracy. "For saying the *F* word."

Nancy spit out a hunk of Hockey Puck. "You said the *F* word to your father?"

"Not to him. Near him."

"I'd be pounded into butter," Tiff said.

"My parents don't really give a flying crap what I do," said Robin, dipping her Hockey Puck into a pool of ketchup. "As long as we don't burn the house down, whatever we do is okay by them."

"Lucky," said Tiff. "What about you, Abigail?"

"She probably never got in trouble in her life," Heather said. "My parents take away my TV."

"You have your own TV?" Robin couldn't believe it. "You're spoiled."

"Just because you have nice things doesn't mean . . ." Heather whined.

"So, did you, Abigail?" Tiff asked. "Get in trouble?"

"Could somebody pass the peanut butter?" Tracy asked, after a quick glance at Abigail, her best friend, the only one who seemed as careful and tense as she felt herself. Abigail was chewing on her lip nervously. "I don't know what these things are, but they taste like boogers," Tracy said.

"I'll take yours," said Tiff.

"You would." Tracy tossed her Hockey Puck like a Frisbee over to Tiff, then smiled at Abigail.

"So?" Tiff asked Abigail, with a mouth full of half-chewed Hockey Puck. "Did you ever get in trouble?"

Abigail thought of something. "One time last year," she said, "I fell asleep with Silly Putty after my mom told me I wasn't allowed to use it in bed, and it got stuck all over me, ruined my pajamas, and we had to throw out the sheets, too."

"She must've been so pissed," Tiff said, smiling.

"Yeah, but here's the thing. I said to my mom, 'Don't get mad,' and she said, 'I'm not mad, I'm angry. Only dogs get mad.' So I'm like, 'That's what I mean, don't get mad.' "

"Oh, snap!" yelled Dana.

"I'd get the wooden spoon right across my face," Tiff said. "What did she do to you?"

"She just said she wanted me to think about how saying that made her feel."

"That's it?"

Abigail shrugged.

"Your mother never hit you in your whole life?"

"She's a pacifist."

"How do you know if you were bad, then?"

Abigail thought about it for a few seconds. "I don't know."

"But when your father got home, he must've smacked the jelly out of you, right?" Tiff asked. "God, my dad's belt would be off so fast, his pants wouldn't have time to fall down before he was whacking me."

"My dad's dead," said Abigail.

Nobody said anything for a minute, and Abigail started to regret blurting it out like that. Aunt Yvonne had told her you're supposed to say he passed on or he's departed, but that just sounded to Abigail as if he took a train to another town.

"I'm sorry," said Kat.

"Thank you," Abigail answered.

"If you need to talk . . ."

"Thanks."

"Hey." Kat banged the table with the palm of her hand, and the campers jumped. "Who ended up winning the jacks tournament?"

"I did," said Dana.

"Tst," said Heather.

Robin slugged her on the arm and whispered, "Shut up, jerk."

Heather said "Tst" again, but very quietly.

"Yeah," Tiff said. "Dana won."

Dana smiled at Tiff. "I'm a premier jacks player."

July 20.
again

Dear Mom,

Thanks for the soap. and the pistachios.

I just got them and everybody's fingers are already red except Tiff's She's allergic to pistachio's Could you please send some cookies next time? She says she's not allergic to Oreo's!!! I ate a lot of Pistachio's. Lunch was gross.

Today it rained. We had a jacks Tournament. Good thing you taught me fancies!!!! Now it stopped so we're going down to boating.

xoxoxo♡,

Abby

PS What are Hockey Pucks? (The food) I think chicken but maybe Veal?
PPS I miss being vegetarians w/ you.
PPS Maybe if you don't feel like pottery you could do cooking
PPPS Don't learn Hockey Pucks.

For the first few minutes, Abigail and Dana went around in circles in the middle of the lake. Finally they gave up and stopped paddling. Abigail dipped her foot over the edge of the canoe into the cool, sludgy water and took a deep breath to keep from asking Dana why she would say she was really good at canoeing when she didn't even know how to paddle.

"What was he like, when he was alive?" Dana asked. "Your father, I mean."

"That's not what you're supposed to say." Abigail splashed a little water with her foot. "You're supposed to say 'I'm sorry.' "

Dana hung a foot over into the water, too. "Why? I didn't do anything."

"That's just what you say."

"Oh. I'm sorry."

"Thank you."

"Thank you? I say 'I'm sorry' and you say 'Thank

you'? Aren't you supposed to say 'That's okay' when somebody says 'I'm sorry'?"

"But it isn't okay," said Abigail.

Dana nodded. "Yeah, that's true." She turned sideways so both her feet hung in the water. "But 'Thank you' is a weird thing to say to 'I'm sorry.'"

"My Aunt Yvonne told me that's what you say. I don't know why." Abigail counted the posts on the bridge going over the lake. Fourteen. Three people walking across. Six clouds above them. At her father's funeral, Abigail had spent the whole time counting the flowers in the arrangements flanking the coffin. That's all she remembered from it—counting flowers. Not what the rabbi or Uncle Isaac had said, not her mother's face or Jake's or how it felt. It hadn't felt like anything, really. One hundred thirty-three or thirty-four flowers. Be brave, Aunt Yvonne had told her. You know your father always said to be brave. If you aren't brave, it will be that much harder for your mother.

Dana kicked the water and splashed herself in the face. "You don't like to talk about him?"

Abigail shrugged. She hadn't cried at the funeral, and when Aunt Yvonne kissed her before leaving that night, she said, "Your dad would've been proud of his big, brave girl today." The words had echoed in Abigail's head as she lay silent in her parents' bed, reminding herself that it was now only her mother's, not wanting to leave in case her father was looking for her

51

to tell her it wasn't true, trying to breathe her father's smell off his pillow deep enough into her nose so that it would stay forever. It hadn't worked.

Abigail shifted on the metal canoe seat and tilted her face up to the sun. "Just usually I don't," she said.

"Okay," said Dana, turning toward Abigail and leaning forward with her arms and the paddle across her knees. "Do you want to hear about when I won the Rhode Island State Championship for twirling?"

"Just usually nobody asks, or they say 'When did you lose him,' something like that."

"Did you like him?"

"You're so weird, Dana." Abigail was angry, biting out the words as she did to nobody except Jake, when he sat on a new box top or wouldn't leave her alone. "Why can't you be normal? That is not a normal question. He's my father." The anger disappeared. Abigail felt exhausted and sorry to have to correct herself. "Was, I mean."

"So? Sometimes I like my father, sometimes no. Just about the only thing he ever says to me is 'Are you keeping your goals in sight?' There's no rule that you have to like someone."

"One time I got cockamamies," Abigail said softly, almost to herself.

"Is that like lice?"

Abigail turned backward in the canoe so she faced Dana. "No. They're temporary tattoos. They come in

Cracker Jacks. My little brother and I got Cracker Jacks from some, I don't know, relative or something, and when we got home and spilled out all that gross sticky stuff—"

"You don't like Cracker Jacks?" Dana was shocked. "I live for Cracker Jacks."

"I hate them. But anyway . . . " Abigail was impatient to get on with the story she had completely forgotten until that moment. "My brother got a good prize, a ring or something, and I got this little book of nothing, like drawings, I thought. I almost threw it away. But I showed my dad first, and he started going, 'Cockamamies! You got cockamamies! Cockamamies, cockamamies!' "

"He sounds like a nut," Dana said.

"Yeah." Abigail smiled to herself, picturing her father happy and silly and so full of life. All her thoughts of her father recently had been of an empty space he should be filling, or, at most, his look of disappointment when she had been too frightened to have fun with him. She had forgotten how silly he could be.

Tracy and Tiff pulled up alongside them in a battered canoe. "Hey, you guys wanna race us to the bridge?" Tiff asked.

"Nah," said Abigail.

Tracy looked into Abigail's eyes. "Oo-yay ure-shay?"

"Yeah, thanks," Abigail said, then added, "Anks-thay."

53

Tiff splashed Abigail with her paddle. "Ater-lay! Come on, Acy-tray, let's see if we can capsize Robin's kayak."

When they were gone, Dana said, "They think I don't know ig-pay Atin-lay."

"Yeah." Abigail ran her hand over the smooth wood of the paddle.

"You're the only one in the bunk who likes me, really, or at least the only one who's like me."

"I know," Abigail said quietly. "Fancy comforters, and everything."

"Yeah. Lots of stuff. So anyway, what happened with the cockamamies?"

"Oh. He got a cup of water," Abigail said, wondering what stuff. She didn't know if she liked Dana, and she definitely didn't want to *be* like Dana. But she was too eager to relive that spring afternoon with her father alive and silly in the living room to waste time worrying. "And he dipped the little pieces of paper in, then stuck them to our hands. He covered me and Jake with them, and told us not to tell Mom because she might get angry. I don't know why. She never gets angry. And besides, it's not like she wouldn't see them. I mean, we were covered."

"Just to make it fun." Dana nodded, excited.

"Yeah." Abigail nodded, too. "Then we went dancing around the house—you can sort of do laps in my house, you know, out one kitchen door, through the dining room and living room, and back in the other side of the kitchen. We were like our own little parade, waving our arms around, yelling, 'Cockamamies! Cockamamies! Cockamamies!' "

Abigail put her hands up over her head the way she and Jake and her father had done that day. The canoe rocked, and Dana almost fell out. She grabbed on to the sides. "Sorry," said Abigail.

"That's okay." Dana picked her hands up, too. "Cockamamies! Cockamamies!"

"Yeah. Well, anyway." Abigail took a breath. "Your father really asks you if you're keeping your goals in sight?"

"Yeah," Dana said, banging her oar on the water. "And I say yes, every time."

"And are you?"

"I don't have any goals, really. I'm not that sure what he means."

Abigail nodded.

Dana touched the water gently with the edge of her oar and said, "I'm sorry he died."

"Me too," Abigail whispered. "I mean, thank you."

July 21

Dear Mom,

I haven't taken off ~~Dadd~~ my Red Sox cap all summer so far. (Except, swim and showering) It's my <u>thing</u>. Tracy has orange sneakers with red laces as her <u>thing</u>. I wish my <u>thing</u> were that I'm brave and daring like ~~to~~ Tilb is. I'm not, tho. I'm trying but when everybody else is doing something daring, like hiding from somebody, I get scared + feel bad. Do you think when I grow up I will be? (Daring) Or will I always be a wimp?

Gotta go
Abby

SWAL'CAKWS...!!!
sealed with a lick cause a kiss won't stick!!!

Sorry about your father," Tracy whispered to Abigail at the sinks as they got ready for Evening Activity. They were going roller-skating, so they had decided, together, to wear loose jeans and their hair down.

"Thanks," Abigail said. She had to smile as she spit out her toothpaste. Tracy knew how to do it, the sorry–thanks routine.

Tracy licked her finger and touched it lightly to her curling iron. "I know it's not the same, but last year my dad moved out for three and a half months."

"That's pretty bad, too, I guess," said Abigail. She wasn't sure what else to do to get ready for roller-skating, so she washed her hands again with the Dove her mother had sent.

"It was horrible." Tracy brushed a section of hair, then rolled it around her curling iron and stood with one foot on top of the other. She spoke into the mirror, to Abigail's reflection. "The house was so quiet without all that fighting. The only noise was Bubby, sighing."

Abigail nodded and dried her hands on her towel.

"Want me to curl your bangs under?"

"That's okay." She tucked her T-shirt in and bloused it. "I think they're still too short."

"Your mom didn't get mad when you cut them?" Tracy asked.

"Angry." Abigail balanced her right foot on top of the left, as Tracy was doing. It was more comfortable than it looked.

"Right—angry." Tracy laughed and rolled up another section, farther back.

"No, not really," Abigail whispered, leaning forward onto the sink. "She said it's *my* hair."

"You think she could adopt me?"

Abigail smiled at her.

"How long ago did he, you know, pass away?" Tracy touched the hair wrapped in the curling iron carefully, as if it were an important scientific experiment. When she released it and it bounced down to her shoulder, she frowned at it slightly. "Your father. Unless you don't want to talk about it. Which is fine."

"Two years and five months, almost." Abigail watched Tracy avoid looking at her. Everybody except Dana always looked down, away, when her father's death came up, and changed the subject as quickly as possible. Abigail did it herself, when her mother couldn't open a bottle of champagne last New Year's Eve and started to cry and said, "I just miss him so much sometimes it hurts my bones." It was the first time she had mentioned him since the Salvation Army took his clothes away in a big red truck. Abigail had been afraid that if she hugged her mother, she would start crying, too, and never be able to stop. So she hadn't moved from her chair. She had clenched her jaw shut and watched the ball drop on TV while her mother went upstairs to take a bath.

"Wow," Tracy said, because she couldn't think of anything else to respond. She'd never met a kid with a dead parent before.

"Yeah," said Abigail. She smiled in her most reassuring way to Tracy in the mirror.

"Listen," Tracy whispered. She unplugged the curling iron and leaned against the sink to face Abigail. "I'm sorry I said that stuff about Bubby and the microwave to you."

"It doesn't matter. My dad didn't die from a microwave."

"But still." She handed Abigail the brush, as a gesture of apology.

Abigail brushed her hair and stuck her Red Sox cap back on. Aunt Yvonne, wedging a black sunbonnet onto Abigail's head for the funeral, had told her that she had a good face for hats. Abigail looked in the Camp Nashaquitsa mirror and hoped it was true. "You think I'll get any M&M's tonight?"

Tracy smiled, relieved. "Definitely."

Abigail was happy the subject was changed, too. "Because," she whispered to Tracy, "so far going out isn't that different from not knowing each other."

"What do you say, ladies?" Kat yelled. "Are we going, or are we primping all night?"

Ten buses were parked on the upper field of Boys' Side, ready to take all 267 campers roller-skating. Jake was waiting for Abigail in front of the first bus.

"What do you say, Jake?"

"Thank you," he said.

"No," Abigail said. "That's an expression."

"Oh."

"Never mind." Abigail looked around but didn't see any friends. "How's camp?"

Jake shrugged.

"Did you write to Mommy yet?"

"Uh-uh." They boarded the bus together. Abigail would've tried to sit with Tracy or maybe Scott, if Jake weren't attached to her again like static cling.

"Jake, you have to write to her. It's really important," Abigail reminded him. "It's the first time she's all alone. You have to write."

"Okay, okay."

"And tell her everything is fine so she won't worry."

Jake sat beside her on the dark green vinyl seat and didn't say a word.

"Okay? Jake? Answer me."

"Okay. I wish I could come stay in your bunk."

"Jake. And remember to tell her you're having fun."

"What if I'm not?"

"Maybe you have to try harder. But if you don't tell Mommy you're having fun, she'll worry. You don't want her to worry, do you?" Abigail put her feet up on the seat in front of them. It was tall, so the heads of the campers didn't show over the top.

"Nobody . . . Everybody . . . " Jake slumped down, tearing with one hand at his cuticles on the other. "The only time I'm included is when we play POJ."

"What's POJ?" Abigail asked, figuring it was a computer game but not really caring much. She was looking out the window for Scott.

"P.O.J. Pile On Jake, and it hurts." He lifted the front of his shirt and showed Abigail a bruise on his belly. "Did you ever hear of that game?"

"No."

"It's not fun if you're Jake."

Abigail saw out the window of the bus that Scott and Caleb were looking around with their hands in their pockets, just like at the past two Brother-Sister

Nights. She turned to Jake and touched his bruise. "Whatever doesn't kill you makes you stronger. Remember Daddy used to say that?"

Jake shook his head. "I don't remember."

"Well, it's true. You have to try not to be wimpy. Laugh it off."

"But it's not funny."

The bus snorted and pulled out. Abigail watched Scott and Caleb board another bus with Robin and Tiff, and wished she could be with them. As the bus passed below the Camp Nashaquitsa sign, it hit a bump that sent Abigail's head pounding into the window.

Scott was loping toward her. Abigail bent down to tie her second skate, but kept watching his legs. He took such long steps it looked as if his body were rushing to catch up. Caleb is cuter, she thought, but Scott looked okay, very tall. Sort of like Gumby. It would be interesting to watch him skate.

"Um," said Scott. He stuck his hands deep into his shorts pockets. "Um," he said again.

"Hi," said Abigail. "This is Jake, my brother." Maybe Scott could act like a big brother to Jake, Abigail thought. Maybe Jake could imitate Scott and learn to be less wimpy. She wished Jake were more like Scott. Then she remembered that she didn't even know what Scott was like. So far all he'd ever said to her was "Um."

"Um," said Scott again.

"Jake," said Abigail. "Do you know Scott?"

Jake shook his head and bent over to pull his skates on.

"Aren't you getting skates? What if they run out of your size?" Abigail asked Scott. She tried to stop herself, afraid she was sounding like Dana. She felt nervous with him standing there waiting for she didn't know what.

"I have big feet," Scott said quietly. "They won't run out."

"Oh," said Abigail. "That's great."

"Really?" He looked surprised.

"Yeah, you know," said Abigail. "For balance." She considered running into the ladies' room to hide for the rest of the summer so she wouldn't have to face Scott after such an embarrassing statement, but she was afraid that if she stood up on her skates she might land on her behind. She pulled the laces of her right skate instead, until her fingers started turning blue.

"Do you, um . . . " Scott looked over his shoulder to the line at the refreshment stand. Caleb was waving him over. "Want anything?"

"That's okay," Abigail said. She blushed, realizing that this was an important moment. Their relationship was becoming official.

Scott looked down at Jake. "You?"

Jake nodded. "A Dr Pepper."

Abigail wished the floor would swallow her up.

Why didn't he know to say "That's okay"? "Well, I'll get you one later, Jake."

"I don't mind," Scott said. "But I'll, um, do you want something, too?"

"No, it doesn't matter."

Scott ran with his hands still in his pockets over to Caleb, whose cute dimples Abigail could see, even all the way across the skating rink lobby.

"You're supposed to say 'That's okay,' " Abigail told Jake.

"But he asked if I wanted something, and I did."

"Never mind." Abigail looked around for other girls from her bunk but didn't see anybody except Nancy, who was already skating around the rink, holding hands with her boyfriend, Rudy. They looked very cute together, their ears so little and pinned back against their heads. Abigail pulled her cap down over her own sort-of-large ears. Uncle Gary waved to her as he skated by, grinning, and said, "Send my regards to Nora in Wayland!"

Abigail waved back and called, "Thanks," then whispered to Jake, "Do you want to introduce me to any of your friends?"

"No." He still had only one skate on. His slow pace made Abigail feel like shaking him. "I'm not having a great summer."

"I can tell," Abigail said, and put her arm around

him. "Maybe you need to find an activity you're interested in, like arts and crafts or rocketry."

"Maybe rocketry," Jake said, his face brightening. "Maybe I'll pick that for elective instead of soccer. Nobody kicks me the ball anyway, and it gets really boring."

Abigail watched Scott lope toward them. She bent down and tied Jake's second skate. "That sounds like a great idea," she whispered.

"Um," Scott said, holding out a can of Dr Pepper to Jake.

"What do you say, Jake?" Abigail prompted.

"Is that just an expression this time or do I say thank you?" Jake whispered.

Abigail smiled as best she could up at Scott. "He's just kidding."

"Thank you," Jake said.

Scott dug into his shorts pocket and pulled out a Chunky, which he held toward Abigail. "I, um, didn't know what you wanted."

"Thanks." Abigail stood up and took the Chunky from his hand. Her ring finger brushed against his pointer, which made her wobble. She sat quickly to avoid falling. "A Chunky. That's great."

"You can exchange it. The woman said. If you don't like Chunkys."

"No, I love Chunkys."

"I just thought, girls like raisins. And Chunkys have, um, raisins, but . . . "

"Thanks. No, it's great. I'll save it. For later."

Scott nodded and ran back to his friends just as the announcer called out, "Couples Only skate!" and the lights dimmed to pink.

July 22

Dear Mom,

Hi! How are you? I'm great! Camp is great!!!
I saw Jake last night. He's great, don't worry. My
boyfriend (Scott) was friendly to him. Bought him a Dr
Pepper! Isn't that nice? I'm having so~~oooo~~ much fun!!!
But don't worry I miss you anyway. How are you? Are you
having a good summer?

Please decide to say yes to shaving. It's <u>umportant.</u>

Love and other tennis scores
Abby

tennis ball.

tennis
raquet

me

you

R otate!"

Tracy walked up to the net, next to Abigail. "Boy, I stink." She rolled her eyes and smiled. "So he really gave you a Chunky? That's too weird."

"Yeah," said Abigail. "A Chunky."

The approaching volleyball took Tracy by surprise. It would have shattered her nose if Robin hadn't lunged forward to bump it up and save the point. The ball twirled in the air above them.

Robin shouted, "Abigail! Yours!"

Abigail closed her eyes, lifted her arms, and whispered, "Please." When her eyes opened, the ball was on the other side of the net. A gangly girl named Lori in the front line of Bunk Twelve slapped it with the palm of her hand and giggled when the ball fell to the concrete.

"Good play, Abigail," Robin said, glaring at Tracy. The ball came flying over the net for Tiff to serve.

Robin jumped up, caught it, and yelled at Bunk Twelve, "Under the net for courtesy! Over the net for jealousy!"

The girls from Bunk Twelve giggled some more.

"Hee, hee," Robin said. At home, she usually played sports with Caleb and the other boys and paid as little attention as possible to the names the girls called her. Girls got distracted too easily, worried about hurting the feelings of whoever was losing, thought more about how they looked to one another than keeping the ball in bounds or scoring a point. Boys did their best, played by the rules, and tried to win. Sometimes Robin wished she'd been born Caleb.

Tiff served it hard, and the most athletic girl in Bunk Twelve, Sarah, dived for the ball but bumped it into the woods. She stood up immediately, and although her knee was scraped and bleeding, she headed out of the court to get the ball.

"Sarah is the only cool one in that whole bunk," Tiff said.

Robin nodded and decided to try talking to Sarah later.

Nancy tapped Tracy on the shoulder. "Did you and Oliver go out to the dugout?"

"Yeah," Tracy said, excited that somebody had seen them.

"I thought that was you. Me and Rudy walked half-way there, but I chickened out. I heard they get you out there and kiss you."

"We kissed for fifteen seconds," Tracy said, proudly.

"Woah," said Abigail. "What was it like?"

Everybody crowded around Tracy. "It was like, I don't know. Kissing." Tracy was nervous, since it was more like one-fifteenth of a second. "You know," she mumbled with as much confidence as she could manage.

"I don't know," Tiff said, wearing her biggest smile, worrying that all the other girls would get asked out by August and she'd spend every Evening Activity sitting unattractively in a corner, eating a 3 Musketeers by herself. "Who would kiss me? The only one ever kissed me on the lips was my grandmother, and it was disgusting, and it wasn't fifteen seconds nearly."

"I have a boyfriend at home?" Dana said. "We kiss all the time. He kisses me, I kiss him, sometimes for sixty or seventy seconds?"

"You should kiss Scott," Tracy advised Abigail, ignoring Dana and desperate to change the subject from how long kisses lasted.

"No thanks," Abigail said, tugging at her Red Sox cap.

"Are we playing or what?" Sarah called from the other side of the net as she whipped the ball under.

Robin nodded at Sarah, caught the ball, and handed it to Tiff. "Eight–six, us."

"I dare you to kiss him," Tracy said to Abigail.

"Eight serving six," Tiff said, and hit the ball directly at Lori, the giggly girl. Lori managed to set it up for Sarah, who spiked it over. Robin bumped it to Abigail, who was caught off guard, thinking about the dare: would the kiss have to last fifteen seconds? How would she know when it was time to stop puckering? On TV they move their faces around a lot. Would Scott want to do that? She wished she'd said something different about herself.

Abigail raised her hands to shield her face at the last possible second. The ball arched over the net and dropped onto the other side like a stone.

"Nice dink!" Robin yelled. She gave Abigail a big smile.

"Thanks," Abigail said, thinking about being chosen first or second, instead of last, next year in gym.

"Dink?" whispered Tracy. She was hoping Abigail wouldn't be angry at her for the dare.

Abigail shrugged her shoulders and smiled at Tracy, imagining going to the Olympics on a volleyball team with Robin. The ball hit her in the legs on its way back to Tiff.

"So you will, then?" asked Tracy. "Kiss him?"

"Scott?" Abigail asked, trying to stall.

"You never say no to a dare, right?"

"I guess I will," Abigail answered, gripping her socks inside her Superstars. She wished she had gotten the smaller size, as her mother had suggested. Her feet hadn't grown yet and the sneakers were too big, too loose, too clunky.

"And then one time?" Dana leaned forward between Tracy and Abigail. "This one time?"

"Nine serving six." Tiff served. Abigail watched the ball sail over and tried to ignore Dana, who kept talking.

"This one time, Danny was really thirsty? And I had a Coke? But Danny hates Coke? Ooo . . . " The ball rushed back, right at Dana, who punched it with her fist and knocked it out of bounds. "Ouch," she complained.

"Hello!" Robin was angry. They were squandering a big lead. "We're playing volleyball here, Dana. Nobody cares about your little boyfriend." Robin ran and picked up the ball.

"So anyway," Dana whispered to Abigail and Tracy. Tracy rolled her eyes at Abigail, who smiled back. "Anyway, I said I would suck off an ice cube for him?"

"You did what?" Tiff asked.

"Six serving nine!"

The ball flew over and Robin spiked it back hard, regaining serve.

"I put an ice cube in my mouth and sucked the Coke off it, and gave it to him. Actually, he took it from my mouth?"

"You sucked his cube?" Tiff walked up to the net. "That's gross. She sucked his cube."

"I'm gonna throw up," said Robin. "Serve, would you?"

Dana took a few steps behind the line and tried a jump serve. It smashed into the net.

"Nice," said Robin.

"Hey, wait, I forgot to say the score. Do I get a second chance?"

"Shut up," said Robin, hurling the ball under.

"That is seriously the grossest thing I ever heard," Tiff said.

"Don't make fun of me," Dana said. "If you don't want certain things told to Kat . . . "

"Six serving nine!"

"I'm not making fun of you," Tiff said. "I'm just saying . . . " She bumped the ball, Heather set it, and Nancy volleyed it back to Tiff.

"That's three," Sarah yelled.

"Duh," said Robin, tossing the ball under.

Heather looked at her fingers and said, "Tst. I hate this stupid game."

"She sucked his cube," Tiff whispered, loudly, to Heather.

"At least somebody besides my grandmother wanted to kiss me," Dana said.

July 23

Dear Mom,

Last night I dreamed I was standing on the high diving board, only it was like incredibly high, not normal high. There was a whole line of people behind me + the pool below me + I was just standing there + standing there + I couldn't move. I kept standing there until my legs were aching + it was night + then I wasn't on the diving board anymore, I was above (!) the ceiling in the playroom — you know — like between the tiles ~~Daddy put it~~ and the real ceiling? And you were calling "Abby? Abby?" + I wanted to scream, "Here I am, Mom! Please help me!!!!" but nothing came out. And then you went away.

Weird dream, huh?!

I'm making you a keychain. Do you like orange? Only 6 days until Visiting Day! Don't forget!!!!!

♡, Abby

P.S. Just kidding — I know you hate orange + wouldn't forget.

Abigail held her palm out for Tiff to fill with shaving cream, then spread the lather on her legs and swallowed hard.

"You better not cut me, Robin," Tiff said, rubbing the shaving cream vigorously onto her shins.

Robin walked toward them, holding her razor in front of her as if it were a weapon. Abigail straightened the straps of her bathing suit and tried to think of a way out of this. Her mother had written that she should wait until after visiting day, when they would discuss it. But she couldn't allow herself to be a wimp. She held her leg up in the air and said, "Ready."

"Put it down, or it'll shake and I'll cut you for sure," Robin said, kneeling beside Abigail. Tiff leaned against the metal shower, which boomed like thunder in response. Abigail jumped. "Stay still!" Robin yelled. "Seriously. It's sharp."

Abigail clenched her teeth and waited. The first

stroke was smooth and soothing, like her mother's hand on her forehead when she had a fever. Abigail let out her breath.

"How does it feel?"

"Good," Abigail told Tiff, surprised.

Dana came into the bathroom, holding her baton, and grabbed the Scope she always left sitting on top of the third sink. "What are you guys doing?"

"Playing chess," Robin said, making the second stroke up Abigail's leg.

"Abigail," Dana said. "Did your mother say yes? I thought you were waiting to get permission."

"You're not in charge of me," Abigail said.

"I didn't say I was," Dana answered, and took a swig of Scope. She watched herself gargle in the mirror, then spit and slammed out the back door with her baton.

"I practice six hours a day," Robin mocked, making a third stroke.

"Ow!" Abigail yelped. The three girls watched a drop of blood bubble up on Abigail's leg, then begin to trail down toward the floor.

"Sorry," said Robin. She ran to the first toilet and grabbed a square of toilet paper, which she stuck onto the bleeding spot. A circle of blood seeped through. "That should stop it." The paper clung to the widening circle of red on Abigail's leg.

"I think we may need to torture Dana," Tiff whispered.

"Watch out or she'll tell about Marco Polo," Robin said, kneeling back down and making a fourth track up Abigail's leg.

"Maybe that's enough," Abigail said, pulling her leg away.

"Once you start ... " Robin answered without looking up from Abigail's leg, which she gripped by the ankle in an attempt to steady it. "Stop squirming and I won't cut you anymore."

"Oh, who cares," Tiff said impatiently. "What did we do, anyway? It was just a game. She banged her toe. We didn't do anything so bad."

As she held her leg still for Robin, Abigail wondered if Tiff was right. It was just a game; Dana had no sense of humor. Just like Dana is not in charge of me, Abigail decided, I am not responsible for protecting her, even if I do secretly like her. "That's true," Abigail agreed. "Why can't she just lighten up and be a kid for once in her life?"

"Exactly," Tiff said. "Doesn't she drive you nuts?"

"Yeah," Abigail said. She couldn't help thinking about the time she and Dana were in the canoe together. "But if you get her alone, sometimes, she can be, I don't know. Pretty okay to talk to. When you get her off the subject of herself."

Tiff laughed. "Which isn't easy."

Abigail tried to chuckle, too, although she had meant to defend Dana.

"You're just pissed because of what she said about you and kissing," Robin told Tiff, to set the record straight. "I don't know why you'd want to kiss a boy, anyway. Their faces are always dirty, and I don't know. Did you ever kiss one, Abigail?"

"Uh-uh."

"Good," Robin said. "None of us did, then. Give me your other leg. Oh, wait. First I have to rinse this off. See?" She held the razor up to Abigail's eyes and showed her the little hairs and soap crud stuck in the blade.

Abigail turned away, saying, "Yuck."

"But now you have to kiss Scott, right?" Tiff asked her.

"I guess, yeah." Abigail touched her shaved leg. It felt smooth and cool and sexy. Embarrassed, she stood up quickly and said, "I don't think Dana means to be nasty."

Tiff bent down and wiped a glob of shaving cream off her foot.

"She just, maybe . . . That *was* a pretty lousy thing to say about you, though, about only your grandmother would kiss you."

"Not that it's untrue," Tiff said.

"I bet somebody else would."

"Some desperate, ugly boy." Tiff smiled to show she could take a joke. Nobody was going to beat her to the punch; she would punch herself bloody and unconscious before anybody else had a chance. She couldn't help wondering if long-legged, athletic Robin and cute little Abigail secretly agreed with Dana, that nobody would ever want to kiss her. The thought made her angry at the world. She laughed and said, "Some fat, pimply-faced loser, right?"

"No, I mean . . . " stuttered Abigail.

"Anyway," said Tiff, shoving Abigail more gently than she truly wanted to, to show she was just kidding around. "It's not just that. I can take a joke. She's just so . . . annoying."

"My IQ is one-forty-five?" Abigail said, imitating Dana. Not nice, she told herself. But Robin toppled over, cackling, and Tiff was knocking her head on Abigail's shoulder, laughing so hard. Abigail knew that being mean was what Tracy liked best about her, too. Maybe the girls at home would notice her if she acted nastier. Trying to be nice mostly meant she ended up playing board games with Jake more than she wanted to, while the other girls in her grade went to one another's houses. She liked to stay at her own house better anyway, she had always told herself. But maybe somebody would ask her to come over if she acted malicious? "One-forty-five?" Abigail was repeating when Dana walked through the bathroom on her way back into the bunk.

"Is it six hours already?" Robin asked, starting on Abigail's second leg.

"Time flies," Tiff muttered, and the three of them laughed as hard as they could all over again. Abigail concentrated on keeping her leg still at the same time.

When they were laughed out, Tiff squatted and whispered, "I say we collect whatever blood you can get out of Abigail's scrawny legs, wipe it on one of Kat's tampons, and tell everyone it's Dana's."

"That's disgusting," said Robin. "Think of something else."

"Don't you want to torture her?" asked Tiff.

"No, I do." Robin wiped the razor on her shorts and then looked at Tiff. "Just, some torture is fair and some is not. That's all."

"I never met anybody so straight." Tiff stood up, shaking her head at Robin but still smiling.

"Shut up," Robin said, knocking her elbow into Tiff's knee.

"How about . . . hang her bra from the flagpole."

"She doesn't have one," Abigail said, before she could stop herself. She hadn't meant to reveal that she knew who had bras and who didn't.

Robin flicked the razor. "Nothing to do with development."

"Development?" mocked Tiff. "Nothing with *development?"*

"Whatever." Robin blushed. "Nothing with ... " She couldn't find another word.

"We could just ignore her," Abigail suggested. "That would be funny."

"Hysterical," said Tiff, folding her arms across her chest. She wondered if Robin and Abigail were really on her side, or if eventually they would dump her, because she was too big and ugly, and choose Dana instead. All three of them were girls without bras, Tiff reasoned; that could be a bond, a club.

"There." Robin shaved the final line of foam off Abigail's leg. "Rinse 'em and see how you like it. Tiff? You're up."

Abigail turned the shower on. She felt the water with one hand and adjusted the knobs with the other until the temperature was right. While she rinsed, she thought about asking Dana to be partners again at canoeing and also about jokes to play on her even though Dana was the first person who ever asked what her father was like.

Abigail wanted to be the kind of person who played practical jokes. She didn't know why she felt so serious all the time. She could hear her father teasing her mother about never knowing how to relax, and that she was teaching Abigail to be tense, too. "Don't you want her to have a sense of humor?" Abigail remembered hearing her father ask Mom. "Why are you making her such a wimp?"

Abigail rubbed her legs clean of soap and watched the square of toilet paper chase itself down the drain. Her legs felt sexy; she couldn't help it. She rubbed them against each other and hoped her mother wouldn't be disappointed.

July 27

Dear Mom,

    Would you love me no matter what?

    Just wondering.

    Love,

    Abby

You want to go to the dugout?" Abigail was staring at Scott's sneakers, Stan Smiths, counting the shoelace holes while she waited for his answer.

"Um," he said.

Tracy and Oliver walked past them, with their arms around each other. Tracy had a bag of peanut M&M's in her other hand.

"If you want to," Scott finally said.

They walked side by side out the back door of Olympic Hall, across the wet dark fields, to one of the dugouts. There were couples on both ends of the bench inside. Abigail didn't want to stare, but she was fairly sure they were kissing.

"Um," Scott said.

Abigail sat down in the middle of the bench. Scott sat down next to her. She turned her Red Sox cap backward, so it wouldn't bump him in the eyes during the kissing.

"Do you . . . " he started to say, but by the time Abigail realized that he was facing her just to talk, not kiss, she was already kissing him. She had her lips puckered like a rosebud, the way Tracy had shown her, and was pressing them on Scott. It wasn't exactly the center of his mouth, she felt. She opened her eyes. He was staring at her. She was kissing the corner of his mouth, plus some cheek. He wasn't doing anything, not puckering like a rosebud or moving his head around or anything. Just staring.

She backed up and returned her cap to its normal position.

He looked out at the field.

She wondered how many seconds the kiss had endured.

He banged the heels of his Stan Smiths against the concrete floor of the dugout.

She watched him bang them.

After about a hundred bangs, he said, "You want to go in?"

"Yeah," said Abigail.

"Scott wants to break up with you," Robin said halfway across the bridge.

"Oh," said Abigail.

"Are you gonna cry?"

"No."

"He's dumping you?" Tracy caught up with them. "After you went to the dugout tonight and everything?"

"That means he was just using you," Tiff explained to Abigail. She had slowed down to walk with them, too.

"You should've broken up with him, first," Heather said from behind Tracy. "What a jerk."

"Thanks, you guys," Abigail said. This was the sisterhood she had always craved at home: the hard knot of girls, whispering agreement, nodding, convincing one another that anyone opposing them was not only wrong, but worthless. And yet, here in the center, the core of the knot, Abigail felt choked.

She wished she could call her mother, but worried that it was too late. She wanted to break away from this gang of girls and run back to use Uncle Gary's phone, which was allowed only in an emergency. Abigail doubted that Uncle Gary would understand that being suffocated with false comfort could be a real emergency.

"Did he say why?" Tracy asked Robin. "I can't believe it." Tracy shook her head at Abigail, trying not to show her relief at still having a boyfriend.

"I don't know," said Robin. "Not really. Scott told Caleb, and Caleb told me to tell her."

"If you want," offered Tracy, "I can ask Oliver to find out."

"That's okay," said Abigail. "It wasn't really going that well."

"He was sort of dorky-looking, anyway," said Heather, wondering if perhaps Scott had become interested in her. She was searching for her true love, and so far he hadn't turned up at Camp Nashaquitsa.

"Yeah," Abigail agreed. "I guess he was dorky-looking."

"He walked funny," Tracy said.

"Sort of *boingy*." Abigail imitated his walk. Too bad if that's mean, she thought, and hoped he hadn't told Caleb and Caleb hadn't told Robin that she kissed him like that, before he was ready and on the corner of the mouth.

"Yeah." Tiff laughed, and imitated his lope, too. "Yuck."

"Maybe he didn't like going to the dugout with you," Dana said.

"Oh, that's nice, Dana." Tracy put her arm over Abigail's shoulder, protectively.

"What did you say, one-forty-five?" Tiff stopped in front of Dana and turned around. Everybody stopped walking except Nancy and Kat, who were behind.

"Just, maybe he didn't want to kiss. No offense. Maybe he didn't like the peer pressure."

"What planet are you from?" Tiff took a step closer to Dana, forcing Dana to arch backward.

"Let's pick up the pace, ladies. . . . " Kat gave Tiff

a little nudge and kept going. Tiff started walking toward the bunk again, so everybody else did, too. Abigail just wanted to slip between her flowered sheets and write to her mom.

"She practically forced him into it, is all I was saying," Dana mumbled.

"I'm sure that makes Abigail feel great, after he dumped her," Tracy said. Abigail trudged along with the group, not saying anything, trying to calculate how many minutes until this night, and then this summer, would end.

"Yeah," Nancy added as they got to the cabin door. "You're making her feel like a real jerk, right, Abigail?"

"It doesn't matter." Abigail sat down on her bed, not ready yet to change out of the soft blue blouse that her mother had bought her in case there was a night she needed to look especially pretty. "I didn't really like him that much, anyway." She peeked at the Chunky on top of her cubby, glad she had saved it to remember him by.

"Was he a good kisser, at least?" Tiff hung her head down from the top bunk to ask. Abigail watched Dana walk quickly past, into the bathroom.

"Put it this way," Abigail said. "I'd rather kiss your grandmother."

While everybody was laughing, Abigail went to find Dana. She was in the second stall, so Abigail went into the first and closed the door.

"Dana?" she whispered.

No answer.

"Dana?"

"Leave me alone."

"I think you're right, possibly." Abigail waited, sitting with her jeans still up, on the toilet, until she felt ridiculous. "About Scott." No response. She stood up. "I don't think he really wanted to kiss."

"I didn't mean to make you feel like a jerk," Dana said. She tried to spit the words out so the tears behind them wouldn't be heard. Her mother always told her to ignore the kids at school when they called her Corroded, but ignoring them, knowing that only metal can be corroded, didn't help. She had hoped camp would be a fresh start, but her corroded personality was obviously inescapable.

"I know you didn't," Abigail whispered from the other stall. "I feel like a jerk all by myself."

"Thanks." The back door creaked open and slammed shut, which jolted Dana. She tried to think quickly of something to say to bind Abigail to her, to make Abigail want to be her friend. "If you want, I could teach you to twirl the baton. Did I tell you I won first place in Rhode Island?"

"No thanks." Abigail left the stall without flushing and went out the back door.

Dana didn't understand what she had said wrong; her parents seemed to like her in direct proportion to how many blue ribbons she acquired. But it was clear to her, alone there in the stall, that she had failed again.

Outside the back door, Kat was lying on the ground looking up at the sky, thinking about her kids. Abigail sat down on the step, not seeing Kat, and rested her head on her knees.

"You're my favorite camper," Kat said quietly.

Abigail jumped. "What?"

"For stuff like that," Kat said, still looking straight up. "You know, for making the effort to be nice to Dana. For realizing she doesn't mean to be irritating. It's good. I like to see that."

"Thanks," Abigail said, letting the idea of being Kat's favorite wash over the rejection from Scott. "She really is irritating, though." Abigail leaned back to look up at the stars, too.

"That she is," agreed Kat.

July 28

Dear Mom,
Hi! How are you? I'm fine. Camp is ~~great~~!!
~~really from~~ ~~different from~~

By the time you get this it will be after Visiting Day
so you'll already know I ~~shaved~~ and ~~either~~ be disappointed in
me or ~~no~~. We will have talked about Arts & Crafts and volleyball
but not about real stuff like what happened tonight + why (????)
By the time you get this it will be ~~too~~ late. So I'm
not gonna send it.
    Since you'll never read this, maybe I can tell the truth.
    Lots is going on this summer that you don't know
about. You think I'm a "happy camper," just a good little
kid. If you only knew.
        Tomorrow when you look at me will you see that
I'm different? What if I'm unrecognizable to you? What
if you don't even notice? (the changes in me) What if you don't
like how I'm turning out? ~~Will you still love me~~
        There's stuff I wish I could ask you but I can't, like:
① What is my IQ?   ~~~~ like
② Do you think Daddy would ~~like~~ me now?

                                    (OVER ⇒ ⇒ ⇒)

He never knew me as an 11-year-old. If being dead is like being asleep maybe he's _not_ watching over me like Aunt Yvonne said (if he is - would he know I'm at camp? Maybe he can't find me?) Maybe instead he's dreaming of me but in his dreams I'm a wimpy little 8-year-old afraid of the dark + high dives + cats + strangers. He'll never know I grew out of needing my Donald Duck nightlight + being afraid to go away from you. But I d̶i̶

My friends here, you don't even know what they look like. (yet.) You don't know their parents or their houses. You don't know that Heather says "tst" or that Dana makes everything into a ? or why one is cool and the other is the most ~~annoying~~ irritating thing!!! You don't know what we did to Dana or why I didn't stop it even tho maybe she is more like me than anybody else here. I don't know why myself or even if I should've or if I should just 'lighten _up_ + be a _kid_ for on like Daddy always used to say. Like when he was a kid + on a Dare he hit all those mailboxes with a baseball bat. (I would never do that.)

Sometimes everything isn't _great_!!! I wish I could talk to you about the things that a̶r̶e̶n̶'t̶ but then you'll wo̶r̶ry + that line between your eyes gets deep + it's my fault, which I can't stand. I know it makes you happy to hear everything is great so I L̲I̲E̲ and tell you Everything is great!"' So much fun!!!!!!|||||||||||| ☺

    I miss Daddy. I miss you. Every night I think what if you die ~~too~~? Jake and I would be orphans. I would take care of him. Don't worry, Mom. I could. Maybe I'm not doing such a great job~~ob~~ looking out for Jake like you said the night before camp I should. I'm trying. I'll try harder.

      Please don't die. I never step on a crack if I can possibly help it.

    ~~I wish~~ I know Daddy didn't like me much. I know he loved me + everything. Parents have to love their kids automatically I think. That's not what I mean. I just think he wanted somebody ~~more~~ different. Honestly. The truth is he was disappointed. But if he can see me now, here at camp, + !!, maybe I can show him I'm different now, ~~and then he~~ I just ~~wish~~
       (I don't even know what I wish.)
       ~~Abby~~ Abigail

Just as Abigail was pouring syrup over her pancakes, Dana's parents arrived. Her mother burst into the dining hall, yelling, "Dana!" and flinging her bangled arms wide. Startled, Abigail dripped some syrup onto the table. Dana blushed and looked down into her lap for a second, but then wiped her hands on her napkin, smiled, and ran into her mother's embrace. Abigail couldn't stop staring at Dana's handsome father. He was wearing a blue suit and a burgundy tie even though it was already over eighty-five degrees and not yet nine in the morning. He leaned against the doorframe, holding a Bloomingdale's bag in each hand. Abigail wondered if he had brought Dana presents he had chosen himself. He looked critically around the room as if he were the Secret Service on guard for somebody trying to assassinate Dana. Abigail smiled at him, but he didn't respond, and when she tried to look casual, she plopped her elbow into the puddle of syrup.

Dana dragged her mother over to the table and introduced each girl and Kat, who stood up to shake hands and tell Mrs. Gold what an enthusiastic daughter she had. Mrs. Gold draped her arms over Dana's shoulders, cuddled Dana close, and said, "That's my baby!"

"No wonder Dana's such a loser," Tiff said after they walked away.

"Give her a break," said Kat. "All parents are embarrassing."

"They aren't supposed to let any of them in until nine," Robin mumbled, helping herself to a fourth pancake.

Abigail left breakfast early to get the gel put on her rash at the infirmary. On her way down the slope to the field, as she rubbed the gel in well so that her mother wouldn't be worried, Abigail saw Robin running toward the parking area with Caleb, toward a Saab that held a tall blond mother, a thin bald father with a bushy beard, and two yellow Labradors. She was surprised that Robin had never mentioned having dogs, or a bald father.

The heat stuck to the campers and weighted down the air so that the flag hung wearily against the flagpole as the cars crept into camp. Abigail sifted pine needles through her fingers as she watched the cars from her position between Kat and Tiff, under a tree at the edge of the field. She spotted Jake and expected him to race over and wait with her for their mother, but he waved and turned back to chatter with a fat curly-haired boy. Abigail knew she should be proud and happy, but instead she thought of telling scrawny Jake that he and fatso looked like a "10" standing next to each other, and couldn't he find any normal friends?

Tracy joined Abigail in playing with the sticky, dead pine needles until she perked up suddenly, pointed, then slammed her hand down onto her thigh, and whispered, "That's them, mine. My parents. And Bubby. Oh, jeez. I asked them not to bring her." She dropped her head into her hands. "It's too hot for her—she'll keep pretending to faint all day." She stood up and dusted off the back of her shorts. "You want to come meet them?"

Abigail shook her head. "I don't want my mom to worry, you know. If she can't find me."

Heather jumped up abruptly and ran toward a black car, screaming, "*Eeeee*! Mommy!"

The woman who emerged from the passenger side of the car wore a hot pink sundress over a tanned, toned body. "Well, hello, little miss!" she called toward Heather, and then snapped at the driver, Heather's father, "Could you wait until I'm out? Is it too much to ask? Tst."

Tracy and Abigail smiled at each other. Tracy said, "Well ... "

"Go ahead. I'll meet them at softball."

Tracy ran toward the parking lot. Abigail scanned the area for Jake but couldn't find him. She turned back to smile at Tiff and Kat, but never completely let her eyes leave the procession of cars rolling somberly under the Camp Nashaquitsa sign, the cars with other kids' parents in them, none of them carrying her own soft-haired, Birkenstocks-with-socks-wearing, oatmeal-and-milk-smelling mother.

"My mother's always late," Abigail told Kat and Tiff. "She was so late picking me up from a birthday party last year I had to play backgammon with the girl's father for half an hour." Abigail had been surprised to be invited to that party, since Eliza Smith was the most popular girl in fifth grade. In her excitement, she had chosen as a gift a bracelet her mother thought was far too expensive and so paid for eight dollars of it out of her own bank account. Then her mother had been half an hour later than any other mother picking up, because she was in the middle of a really good book and lost track of time. Abigail got beaten by Eliza Smith's father at backgammon in the den while Eliza went up to her room to look at her gifts for what seemed like hours. Abigail had never been invited back since, and hadn't even gotten a thank-you note for the bracelet she'd never seen Eliza wear.

"My parents may blow it off totally," Tiff said. "They might."

Kat fanned herself and said, "I doubt it."

Tiff shrugged and tried to smile. "They may. It wouldn't surprise me, and I wouldn't care."

"If they did," Kat said, turning her face to the sun, "you'd get to hang with the counselors. We're sending out for pizzas with the works, if we don't die of the heat first."

Abigail wondered if her mother would completely forget, and decided that if she did, she and Jake would eat pizza with the counselors and then run away from camp and live off the land for a few years until she could get a job and support them and then she'd write a best-seller about her experiences and her mother would be reunited with them on national television, where she would cry and beg the country's forgiveness for forgetting visiting day, but people would line the streets booing her, jeering that her kids deserved better.

Just as she was beginning to try to work out the details of the escape, Abigail spotted her mother's red Honda through the haze. She lifted her cap and brushed the sweaty bangs off her forehead. "You want me to wait with you, Tiff?" she asked without taking her eyes off her mother's car.

"That's okay. I've got Kat."

Abigail headed toward the slow-moving Honda, where Jake was already jumping up and down as he ran alongside, waving a square covered lumpily with blue tiles, yelling, "You're here! You're here!"

Abigail leaned toward her mother to finish the story of her volleyball triumph. "And then Robin said, 'Nice dink!' "

"Nice dink?" Abigail's mother asked her. "I don't know what 'Nice dink' means."

"Me neither," said Jake, plucking a fuzz ball off the picnic blanket and inspecting it.

"Me neither! But boy, was I proud."

Her mother laughed, tucking her short hair behind her ears. Abigail loved to hear her mother laugh, to watch her normally tight face relax and pull back into a grin. Her father's laugh had been so easy, exploding at the silliest jokes, even knock-knocks she made up. Strangers used to turn around in restaurants and not be able to stop themselves from smiling, too. It was a really happy laugh. Mom would get embarrassed and say, "Jerry . . . " and open her eyes wide at him, which just made him say, "Nora . . . " and laugh harder. Mom's laugh was more contained, and harder to come by.

Abigail noticed the family under the tree next to them turning their heads to look. "Mom . . . " Abigail said, opening her eyes wide.

"Abby . . . " Her mother leaned back on her elbows, and looked at Abigail. "What's wrong, Abby? It seems—

not just now but in your letters, too—are you having a hard time here? Is something . . . "

"Everything's great!" Abigail played with the yellow-and-blue lanyard hidden in her shorts pocket and stared at the yellow and blue of the Mexican blanket beneath her. Her mother's favorite colors. "It's just . . . your hair."

"Oh." Mom tucked the hair behind her ear again. "Well, do you like it?"

"Yeah, it's just . . . I mean, it's *your* hair. It's just . . . "

"Different." It was barely touching her shoulders. Before, she'd had to pick it up to sit down.

"Yeah."

"I like it," said Jake. "It's beautiful."

"Well, thank you, Jake."

"No, I like it," said Abigail. "It's just you don't look like, I mean, like a vegetarian anymore."

Mom laughed again. "Well, I still am, underneath."

"Why were you late?"

"I told you, Abby, I had to stop for gas, and then there was just a long line of cars trying to get in here. I wasn't late. Between nine and ten, the thing said, and I was here at quarter to ten. Please don't make me feel terrible all day, Abby."

"You weren't finishing a book?" Abigail mumbled.

"No, Abby. I wasn't." Her mother looked her straight in the eyes, angry and hurt and surprised.

Abigail saw all three feelings mingled and wished she could suck her words back inside. "So," she said. "The drawing class is good?"

"It's great! Mostly it's fun to get out and spend time with other adults, make some new friends. You were right, Abby. It's just what I needed."

"Great," Abby said. "That's really great."

"So," said Mom. She pulled a Tupperware of homemade oatmeal chocolate chip cookies out of her backpack.

Abigail tried again to sound enthusiastic. "My favorites!"

"I know," said her mother, smiling. "And chocolate pudding for Jake."

"You're terrific, Mom," Abigail said, taking a bite. "Mom?"

"Yes, Abby?"

"I shaved."

"I noticed."

The bite of cookie felt like a jagged stone scraping its way down Abigail's insides.

"I made a friend," Jake said, with his mouth full of chocolate pudding. "We both like rocketry. His name is Hank, I'm pretty sure. We choose it for every Free."

"That's wonderful, Jake. Have you made a rocket?"

"Yes. You want to see?"

"Of course I do." She smiled at Jake, then turned and looked at Abigail again.

"Are you angry?" Abigail's hand was sweating on her cookie.

"I'm wondering why you ... Weren't we planning on discussing it today?"

"I couldn't wait!" Abigail threw her cookie onto the Mexican blanket and wiped her hand on her shorts. "I looked like a hairy ape!"

"Where did you get the razor?" Mom handed Abigail a napkin.

"It was Robin's. She did it."

"For you?"

"Yeah." Abigail wiped her hands clean on the napkin and folded it, smoothing all the wrinkles out.

"Did she cut you?"

"Yeah, but it's okay. Just a tiny scab."

"Can I see?" Jake asked. He leaned over to examine Abigail's leg.

"Are you going to shave again?" Mom touched Abigail's leg lightly. Her hand was cool and soft. "Once you start ... "

"True. Well, they look really nice."

"You really think so, Mom?"

Her mother nodded. "You are getting so grown-up I can hardly stand it!" She hugged Jake. "You'd better stay young a few more minutes, Jakey."

"I'm getting grown-up, too," said Jake, pulling away. "Look what I made you." He handed her the blue tiled square he had been lugging around all morning.

"Oh, Jake," said Mom. "I love it. What gorgeous colors of blue you chose!"

"What is it?" Abigail asked.

"It's a trivet. For putting hot pots on. I made it."

"I've been needing a trivet," said Mom. "But I haven't ever seen one so special."

"You mean it?" Jake dropped some chocolate pudding on the blanket, he was so excited.

"The pots will tip," Abigail said, swabbing the pudding with her napkin. "The tiles are all uneven."

"I couldn't get them flat," Jake mumbled. "Other kids got theirs flat."

"Abby." Mom shook her head, then smiled at Jake. "Just flat? How boring. Their poor mothers. This one has . . . topography."

Jake smiled proudly at Abigail. "Yeah, it does, doesn't it?"

Abigail fingered the blue-and-yellow lanyard key chain again, and decided not to give it to her mother. It was just box stitch, not butterfly.

July 29

Dear Mom,

It was *sooo* good to see you today. Thanks for the cookies + the binoculars — you know how long I've been wishing for them!!!

I'm sorry I didn't walk you to the car just now. I *really* wanted to get started on trying to watch birds before it gets too dark. That's why I ran up to Girls' Side. I *wasn't* crying. Don't listen to Jake. Honest. I bent an eyelash into my eye w/ the binoculars is why.

~~Today I~~ ~~Sorry if I~~ ~~Did it seem weird~~ I felt ~~Mom? It~~

I'm glad you didn't get angry about the shaved legs. Were you just saying that, about they looked good? Do you think I'm too young?

You look *great*!!! Your hair. I'm glad your takin a class. I'm glad you like it. This is our summer for FUN!!! I'm glad your takin FUK

I'm having *lots* of FUN !!!!

Gotta Go!!! Out of Space!! Love ya, Abigail

Tracy buried her head in the pillow in her lap. "They *always* do stuff like that!"

Abigail sat down on Tracy's bed and asked, "What happened?"

"Where were you?" Robin asked with her finger in her mouth. In the other hand was a box of Jell-O, torn open at the corner. "Your box is on your bed, Abigail. My mom always brings one each."

"Thanks," Abigail said, and decided she might as well try it. Most of the other girls had red index fingers and seemed happy enough. "What happened?"

Tracy lifted her head off the pillow and looked at Abigail. "How come you weren't at the parent-camper softball?"

"We had to go to my brother's rocketry thing. What, you struck out?"

"Oh, please," Tracy said, and dropped her head back down into her pillow. Abigail opened her Jell-O box and plunged in her finger. It didn't really taste like much of anything. Maybe you need more, she thought, so she tried again.

"Worse than striking out," Robin said.

"Your father struck out?"

Tiff snickered. "You could say that."

"What?" Abigail hated being left out when everybody else knew what was going on. She sucked hard on her finger.

"You may as well hear. Everybody else heard," said Tracy, hugging the pillow. "Let me have a fingerful." Abigail held out her box. Tracy's was unopened on her cubby, but Abigail knew Tracy would probably share hers later, so she didn't mind. "So I'm standing out in center field, and I hear my dad yell, 'Tracy! Tracy!' So I'm like, 'What?' And he goes, 'Bubby has to make!'"

"He said that?" Abigail couldn't believe it. Tracy had her head back in the pillow, so Abigail looked around. All the other girls were nodding.

Robin couldn't hold in her laughter anymore. "Yup! 'Bubby has to make!' Everybody heard."

"I'm never leaving this bunk again," Tracy said into the pillow.

"Maybe people didn't know it was your family," Abigail suggested. "Have some more." Tracy stuck her finger out and Abigail positioned the box of Jell-O around it.

"No," said Nancy. "Everybody knows because she said, 'What?' when her father called her."

"Nancy, you better never tell anybody at home, or you're dead."

"I won't."

"I want to die," Tracy said as she lifted her head for a second to pop her Jell-O'ed finger into her mouth.

"Oh, come on." Tiff came over and sat on Tracy's bed. Abigail made room. "Embarrassing stuff happens to everybody."

"Not this bad," mumbled Tracy. "This is off the charts."

"I bit into a cherry tomato once," Tiff offered.

"So what?"

"So it squirted all over my Uncle Ed."

Tracy lifted her head and smiled a little. "Really?"

"And he was wearing a white suit."

"A bird pooped on my head," said Robin.

"Ew!" Heather yelled. "That is revolting!"

"Yeah, and it was on the way to school the day of school pictures."

"Don McDermot saw me in a towel," said Dana, with a big smile.

"Don McDermot?" Robin squinted her eyes, as if by looking hard enough she'd be able to see if Dana was lying. "*The* Don McDermot? The host of 'Kid Warriors'?"

Dana smiled even more. "He knows this friend of my mother's? My mother is an assistant executive producer at Channel Five, so she knows lots of people who know famous people, and so anyway one day last year? This guy she knows had to stop by our house to pick something up from my mother, and Don McDermot was with him, so they both came in, and I was getting out of the shower, so I didn't know? I heard voices, so I went into the hall in my towel to see who it was and it was Don McDermot!"

"What's so embarrassing about that?" Tracy asked.

"Well," Dana said. "I was, I mean ... "

"You're just bragging," Tiff said. "That's not embarrassing. You just want us all to think you're so great because you met Don McDermot."

"Never mind," Dana said. She wasn't smiling anymore.

"One time," Abigail said quickly, "I was a corncob."

"What?" Tracy started laughing.

"I was a corncob. In a school play. For Brownies, in second grade."

"That's not so bad," said Robin.

"Wait," Abigail said. "It gets worse."

"Worse than being a corncob?" Tracy thought being a corncob was embarrassing enough. She had been the crocodile in her Brownie troop's production of *Peter Pan*, but would never have admitted it.

Abigail looked over at Dana, who was pouring little piles of red Jell-O into her palm and licking them off, and decided it would be better to admit the most heart-stoppingly embarrassing thing that ever happened in her entire life than to admit something only half-embarrassing, half-interesting, and end up feeling the way Dana looked. "Yeah," she said. "Worse. I was terrified. I didn't want to do it. I had to do this little dance...."

"Show us," Nancy begged. Her sister, Ruth, had to perform in a dance recital once and had faked a sprained ankle. Dancing was the one and only thing Nancy felt she was any good at. "Show us the corncob dance."

Abigail stood up and flexed her palms. "You had to start like this...." She shuffled her feet for a second, then flopped back down to Tracy's bed. "I don't really remember."

"Come on," said Heather, sucking on her red finger.

"All I remember is looking out into the seats of the Activity Room, and seeing like thousands of people there, it felt like, and I couldn't remember the dance or what I was supposed to do or the words to the corncob song, so I..."

"You what?" Tracy asked, smiling.

"I started to..."

"To what?"

"To pee!"

"Onstage?" Robin was impressed. She put down her Jell-O box.

Tracy was punching her pillow, laughing. "In your corncob suit?"

Abigail nodded. "And once you start . . . "

"You can't stop!" Tiff shrieked.

"I was peeing and peeing. And crying and crying. I ran off, of course. My mother said nobody would know it was me who had the accident since the whole Brownie troop was in the same costume. And then my dad, to make it worse, couldn't stop laughing."

"Right in front of you?" Tracy grabbed Abigail's box of Jell-O and dug in.

"Yup. He thought it was the funniest thing I ever did." Abigail took Tracy's pillow and buried her head in it. "I quit Brownies, of course."

"A Brownies dropout," Tracy said, laughing.

"Good thing you never tried twirling," said Dana.

Abigail looked across the bunk. "Huh?"

"You have to get up in front of lots of people and do your routine. And poise counts."

"Shut up," Tiff said.

"I'm just saying."

"You're just *bragging*," Robin said. "Don't you know how to be a friend?"

"You're jealous, all of you," Dana said, standing up and grabbing her baton. "I told my mother about

110

you and she said you're all jealous because I have good skin and I've won awards." She stormed out the back door of the bunk as Kat was walking in the front.

"What's going on?" Kat asked.

"Nothing," said Tiff.

"We're just torturing each other," Heather said.

Kat put her Walkman back on. "Oh, good," she said. "That's what I like to hear."

July 29

Dear Mom,

I know I already wrote today but I forgot to tell you how much I like the girls in my bunk. Remember Tiff? The one whose parents were even later than you? Tiff thought they were blowing it off. She ate lunch w/the counselors - they when they showed up (1:30) after a flat tire she ate a whole other lunch w/them. She says it wouldn't've mattered if they didn't come but she was actually I think so happy. She fell asleep hugging the bag of potato chips they brought her.

I told about when I was a corn cob. Do you believe it? But it was OK. It was funny. We all laughed. (Even me!!) Maybe I'm getting to be more that daring. Not like I thought would happen in camp, like survival skills or wild animals, but you know what I mean?

Tomorrow I'm choosing diving + going off the high dive, + also maybe I'll spot a bald eagle!!!!!!!
I love camp. And you. Abigail.

Abigail!"

Abigail had been dreaming that she and Jake were being chased by a bear but that she remembered to lie down and pretend she was sleeping to keep the bear from attacking, so the bear was licking her face, becoming a friend, or a pet, and Abigail thought he was calling her by name. She opened her eyes and saw it was Tiff kneeling next to her, not a bear. She was disappointed.

"Hmm?"

"I figured it out," Tiff whispered. "What to do to Dana."

Abigail nodded and flipped over. She wanted to get back to the dream before she lost it.

"Seriously. Wake up. I need help. It's the best practical joke."

Abigail took a deep breath and turned to face Tiff. The dream was gone. "What?"

"I was just thinking what a jerk she was to you about peeing in your corncob thing." Tiff gently brushed Abigail's bangs off her forehead.

"And to you about boys," Abigail whispered. She looked around the dark bunk. Everybody else was sleeping.

"Yeah, plus about how she thought she was so great because her parents came first this morning, early, all that. But the thing is, I mean, I was thinking about you peeing onstage."

"Don't think about that, do me a favor." Abigail sat up and pulled her blanket over her crossed legs as Tracy always did in the morning while everybody else was getting ready, and wished her eyes were blue like Tracy's.

"And I was thinking, we should do that to her," Tiff whispered, leaning her arms on Abigail's comforter.

"Do what?"

"Pee."

"Huh?"

"In her mouthwash." Tiff smiled triumphantly.

"That's gross."

"Yeah."

Abigail rubbed her eyes. "No. I mean, that's really gross."

"It's a joke."

"It's nasty."

"It's funny. Don't you have a sense of humor?"

"I don't know." It's not that funny, Abigail thought. She wondered if it could be dangerous, and if her father would think peeing in somebody's mouthwash was funny. She knew without wondering what her mother would think. "Maybe we could come up with something better."

"Peeing in her mouthwash is excellent. You're not scared of getting caught, are you?"

"No, not that." She didn't want Tiff—or anybody— to think she was a wimp. "It's just . . . "

"Because everybody's asleep. Nobody will hear. What do you say?"

Thank you, Abigail thought. No, no, that's just an expression. Tiff looked so disappointed. "Do you really think it's good?"

"It's great!"

"It's just . . . " Abigail tried to think of something. Leave Dana alone? That wouldn't work. Leave me alone? Can't take a joke. No sense of humor. Don't be a wimp. "I'm so tired. Let's talk about it tomorrow." Abigail lay back down and pulled the blankets up over her head. She hoped if Tiff decided to go ahead with the joke, she would wake up Robin for help instead. She wanted not to know about it.

"You gotta do it now, or it's no good."

"Wait." Abigail uncovered her face. "Me?"

Tiff smiled. "I dare you."

July 30

Dear Mom,

Maybe instead of an adventurer I'll be a doctor. I'm getting interested in innards. I don't know where my liver is, or pancreas. Don't you think a person by the time she's 11 should keep track of stuff like that? While I was falling back to sleep last night I kept counting my teeth (23) I couldn't stop counting. 23 23 23 with my tongue. I dreamed they were falling out + my internal organs were rotting. I woke up + I'm <u>hollow</u> it feels like. The sun is coming up. Soon everybody will be awake. Now just me. Maybe I should go right now to the infirmary + ask them where is my pancreas + is it OK or rotting.

First I have to get dressed + make my bed + be toilets.

Love,
Abigail

PS Don't worry its probably just allergies

When Abigail saw Dana heading to the third sink and reaching for the bottle of mouthwash, she closed the stall door and stared at the toilet. She put her hands down on the edges of the seat, to keep from falling over. She felt dizzy, as if she had stood up too fast. It was hard to keep her balance with the floor lurching under her.

"What?" She heard Robin yell. "She did what?"

Tiff was laughing. Heather was laughing. Abigail hung on to the walls to keep from drowning.

"Spit!" Robin shouted.

Abigail turned around and opened the stall door in time to see her pushing Dana's head over the sink. Dana was spitting and gagging. Abigail couldn't tell if things were going in slow motion or fast, but they definitely didn't seem normal. She heard Robin telling Dana to rinse out her mouth, and something about pee, and saw Tiff and Heather laughing through their hands near the bathroom door.

"I can't believe you," Robin said to Abigail as she held Dana's head. Abigail looked down.

Tiff and Heather came over and grabbed Abigail. "Excellent," Heather said. Tiff hugged both of them.

Robin pushed Dana past them and out the front door of the bunk. Abigail followed them but stopped at Tracy's bed, where Tracy was lying, reading. She didn't stop when Abigail sat down.

Waiting, Abigail ran her finger over the macramé ankle bracelet Tracy had made her and tried not to think. She started counting stitches, and was up to twenty-one when Tracy said, without lifting her face, "Pretty disgusting."

Abigail nodded. Twenty-two, twenty-three.

Tracy clicked her retainer against the roof of her mouth and stared at Abigail for a few seconds, then whispered, "You really did it?"

"She dared me."

"So?"

Abigail couldn't think of anything to say. Twenty-four, twenty-five.

"Gross," Nancy shrieked. "She swished with piss?"

Heather and Tiff slapped their hands over their mouths and bent over laughing again.

"Abigail did it last night," Tiff blurted out as Kat slammed into the bunk.

"You did this?"

Abigail looked up into Kat's angry face. She tried to swallow but couldn't. She nodded. Kat grabbed the front of Abigail's sweatshirt and yanked her off the bed, toward the door.

"It's just a joke," Abigail heard Tiff say.

"Come with me," Kat said, slowly and quietly. "All of you, come with me." She opened the front door and Bunk Eleven streamed out behind her.

Abigail listened to the ground crunching under her Superstars and tried to breathe in rhythm with the noises. She looked up at Kat, who was shaking her head as she yanked Abigail along, faster and faster, toward the pool. Abigail watched the high dive as she was pulled past it. She dared herself to choose diving at elective and jump off it this afternoon; she told herself she was a wimp if she didn't. But the words clattered in her head and went away. If she jumped or didn't, she thought as she stumbled down the rocky steps beside Kat, it wouldn't make any difference at all.

Kat held the screen door to Uncle Gary's office open and watched her kids file past her, never loosening her grip on Abigail's Camp Nashaquitsa sweatshirt, then shoved her favorite camper in and let the door slam behind them. Uncle Gary sat behind a steel desk, resting his head on his fists, not smiling for the first time all summer.

Abigail looked at each of the dozens of bunk pictures hanging on his wood-paneled walls instead of at him. Row after row of smiling campers in white Camp Nashaquitsa T-shirts. Which ones were the outcasts, and which were okay? It was impossible to tell. Tiff grabbed Abigail's hand and pulled her over. Though she thought she should probably find her own chair, Abigail curled into Tiff's lap. Across the room, Robin and Tracy were staring at their sneakers. Dana's face was covered by her hands.

Uncle Gary leaned forward. "Did you urinate in Dana's mouthwash, Abigail?"

Abigail could see Heather biting down on her lip to keep from laughing at the word "urinate." She felt Tiff let out a puff of hot air on the back of her neck.

"Tiff dared her to do it," said Robin.

"Is that true?" Uncle Gary asked Abigail.

All the campers in the photographs watched her, smiling, waiting.

"It was just a joke," Tiff said.

"Let me get this straight," said Uncle Gary. "Tiffany suggested that you urinate in Dana's mouthwash, and you, Abigail, thought, What a good idea! and went ahead?"

"Not suggested," said Robin. "Dared."

"Thanks, Robin," Tiff mumbled.

"I can't help it," said Robin. "It's the truth. She shouldn't get all the blame."

Uncle Gary was still staring at Abigail. "Why did you do such a horrible thing?"

There was no sound except for Uncle Gary's clock. Abigail was listening to it, trying to figure out what was weird. It doesn't tick, she realized. It only tocks. Tock, tock, tock.

"I don't know," Abigail finally said.

"Answer me."

"I think . . . " Kat started, but Uncle Gary held up his hand abruptly, without lifting his focus from Abigail's down-turned face. Kat wilted silently against the doorframe.

"I'm waiting, Abigail," said Uncle Gary.

Abigail was waiting, too. Waiting for words to come out of her mouth, the room to explode. Nothing happened. Did she really urinate in Dana's mouthwash?

Obviously I didn't, Abigail thought. That is not something Abby Silverman would do. "I don't know." Tock, tock, tock.

"That is an insufficient answer."

Abigail didn't say anything, because she agreed.

"What do you think I should do about this, Abigail?"

"Maybe . . . " Abigail had to stop to clear her throat. She looked across the room to where Robin was staring at her sneakers again, next to Dana, who was still covering her face with her hands. Abigail wished she were sitting on that side of the room. "Maybe you should kick me out of camp."

"Oh, I'm definitely going to do that," Uncle Gary said. "But do you think that is sufficient punishment for what you've done?"

"You could make me use the mouthwash," Abigail whispered.

"It would serve you right," said Kat, attempting to show Uncle Gary some of the toughness she had tried to exert over her kids. "And Tiff, too."

"Tiffany will be docked indefinitely, and moved to Bunk Twelve." Tiff let out another burst of hot air. Abigail realized there was no air in her own lungs. "And, Katherine? Your comments are not helpful."

Kat sank into a chair beside the door. Abigail focused on taking tiny breaths, in-out-in-out, not trusting her body to keep from suffocating without her complete attention.

"What I would like," said Uncle Gary, returning his stony eyes to Abigail, "is an explanation."

Abigail couldn't think of one. "I didn't ... " She gulped some air and continued, "Mean to."

"Are you saying this was an accident?" Uncle Gary's neck was turning red. Red neck, white shirt, blue shorts, Abigail thought. How patriotic. She was having trouble concentrating on anything except breathing in-out-in-out. Her fingers were beginning to tingle. "You *acci-*

dentally took the cap off another camper's mouthwash, you *accidentally* . . . Which part was an accident?"

"The whole thing," Abigail tried to say, but she couldn't tell if she actually spoke the words. Her body was buzzing, it was dots, she was dissolving into atoms and molecules and teardrops. People were standing up and leaving, leaving her alone, millions of unconnected dots, on a cold metal chair watching Uncle Gary, who wasn't her uncle, dial her mother's number on the telephone. It wasn't me, Abigail yelled, but the tocking was so loud no other sound was possible. It couldn't be me, she screamed silently to all the happy campers staring at her, frozen in time on the wood-paneled walls.

July 30

Dear Mom,

Sorry so sloppy but I'm shaking. I'm supposed to be packing—you'll be here soon. I can't yet.

I'm so sorry Mom. You probably are ~~so~~ disappointed You probably will never trust me again or like me. The ~~reason~~ I was trying to ~~be prove~~ I

Its not hate. I like her, the girl I did this to. Dana. I like her. She knows how to be a friend. She was actually my best friend here. Dana.

You should punish me. Whatever you want to do, + I won't complain I deserve it.

Only, could we not tell Jake? Please?! Could we tell him I got sick? We could even tell him I got too homesick + had to call you cuz I can't take it, I was too much of a wimp, had to crawl back to my mother. I don't care. I just don't think I could ever face

"H i," Dana said.

"Hi," said Abigail.

"I came to get my baton. I'm excused from swim, if I want, today, but I have to get right back down there because Kat said she's gonna be much stricter? For the rest of the summer? She practically got fired, you know, because she should've been supervising us better? But he just gave her a warning. Uncle Gary?"

Abigail nodded and set down her pen and box of stationery. "Dana?"

"Is your brother going home, too?"

"I don't think he'll want to. He's having fun. He made a friend."

"That's good."

"Yeah. It is good."

Dana faced her cubby and straightened her things. "Your mom isn't going to hit you with a wooden spoon or anything, is she?"

"She'll probably hug me," Abigail said quietly.

"That's worse, sort of." Dana tore a piece of gum and handed half to Abigail. "Especially if she gives you the look, after."

"The Who Are You look," Abigail agreed, unwrapping her gum. "Yeah, I know. I'd rather be hit. Dana?"

Dana grabbed her baton from its position between her bed and cubby. "You want to see the routine I used to win the Rhode Island State Championship?"

"Sure." Abigail popped the gum into her mouth and placed the wrapper, folded, in her back pocket.

"Okay." Dana stood in the middle of the wood floor and smiled big. "Dana Gold, Barrington, Rhode Island, eleven." She stopped smiling and admitted, "I was nine and a half when I won. The under-tens?"

"Oh," said Abigail.

Dana put the big fake smile back on and started twirling the baton. She's actually pretty good, Abigail thought, relieved and a bit suprised that she could twirl at all. The baton was whirling so fast it was a blur as Dana passed it from hand to hand, behind her back, over her head, all without moving a muscle in her face. The grand finale was a toss up in the air. Dana spun around and lifted both arms, but the baton hit the ceiling of the bunk and clanked to the floor.

"Damn." The smile was gone. Dana picked the

baton up and wound her fists around it, against her chest.

"That was excellent," Abigail said, and clapped.

"Never mind."

"No. Seriously. I didn't know you were that good."

"There's a lot I guess we didn't know about each other."

Abigail chewed on her pen. "Yeah."

"The ceiling at the Civic Center is much higher. Usually I never miss that catch."

"No, I can tell. You're really good. Dana?"

"Yeah?"

"I'm sorry."

Dana looked down at her baton for a while, rubbing it between her palms. "That's okay."

"Is it?"

"No. Not really."

"Do you think you'll ever forgive me?"

"Probably not."

Abigail let out a big breath. "I don't blame you. I wish . . . "

"If wishes were horses, beggars would ride."

"What?"

"I don't know. My father says that."

"I thought all he ever said was 'Are you keeping your goals in sight?' "

"Sometimes he also says, 'If wishes were horses, beggars would ride.' "

"Oh." Abigail nodded again.

"But he has never said, 'Cockamamies, cocka-mamies.' "

Abigail took off her Red Sox cap and held it out to Dana. "You want this?"

Dana shrugged.

"It was my father's."

Dana reached out and took the cap. She put it on her head. "How does it look?"

"Great."

"You sure?"

"Yeah. You have a good face for hats," Abigail said.

"I know I do," said Dana. "But, I mean ... You sure?"

"Oh. Yeah. Remember you asked me that time about my dad? If I liked him?"

"Yeah."

"Sometimes, no."

Dana nodded. "Well ... "

"Well."

Dana swung the baton onto her shoulder. "Gotta go."

"Dana?"

Dana stopped, halfway out the door.

"I really am sorry."

"I know," Dana said. "I mean, thank you."

August 12

Dear Daddy,

It's me, Abigail. That's what I told people to call me this summer. Abigail. Because I know you liked Abigail better than Abby. So I tried it out. I thought, camp. I could start over. I could be Abigail, and brave.

It didn't work out that well.

Do you know that already? Are you watching me? Maybe you couldn't find me before, when I was in camp. I'm back here in my room now, so maybe you can see me again.

Mom said she feels like she hardly knows me, after what I did + I can't explain why. Starting Thursday we're going to a therapist to work out my feelings. She still loves me, though. At least that's what she says.

Do you?

I mean it. I really want to know the truth. This is who I am. Your daughter. Spending August in my room. I have crooked bangs and no

$\longrightarrow$

friends & I'm not scared of the dark anymore Daddy but now I'm scared of other things that a nightlight doesn't help (because they are in me.) I finally got binoculars like you had when you were a kid but I haven't seen anything, ya really.

I know this isn't the exact daughter you wanted, this one that I am. But this is me. I still have never said no to a dare. I'm a wimp. I was thrown out of camp. I'm eleven.

I hate the Red Sox.
I miss your laugh.
~~Abby~~ Abby